LOST IN LION COUNTRY

Another You Say Which Way Adventure
by:

BLAIR POLLY & DM POTTER

ISBN-13: 978-1518815560
ISBN-10: 1518815561

How This Book Works

- This story depends on YOU.

- YOU say which way the story goes.

- What will YOU do?

At the end of each chapter, you get to make a decision. Turn to the page that matches your choice. **P62** means turn to page 62.

There are many paths to try. You can read them all over time. Right now, it's time to start the story. Good luck.

Oh ... and watch out for the hyenas!

Lost In Lion Country

Left Behind.

You only jumped out of the Land Rover for a second to take a photo. How did the rest of your tour group not notice? You were standing right beside the vehicle taking photos of a giraffe. It's not like you walked off somewhere.

The next thing you know, dust is flying and you are breathing exhaust fumes as the Land Rover races off after the pride of lions your group has been following all morning.

"Wait for me!" you scream as loud as you can. "Wait for me!"

Unfortunately, the revving diesel engine drowns out your cries. Surely one of your family members on the safari will notice you are missing. Maybe that nice teacher lady from Chicago you were chatting to earlier will wonder where you are. Won't the driver realize he's one person short?

You smack yourself on the forehead. This will teach you for sitting alone in the back row while the others on the safari sat up front to hear the driver's commentary.

"This is not good," you say to yourself.

What are you going to do now? It's just as well you packed a few emergency supplies in your daypack before you boarded the tour. You have bottled water, a couple of sandwiches, a chocolate bar, your pocket knife and your trusty camera. But these things won't help you if you are seen by hungry lions, leopards, cheetah or one of the other predators that stalk the savannah.

With the vehicle now only a puff of dust in the distance, you notice something else much closer, a pack of hyenas. These scavengers weren't a problem when you were in the vehicle, but now you are on foot and the hyenas are heading your way!

You know from all the books on African wildlife you've read, these dog-like animals can be vicious and have been known to work as a team to bring down much larger animals. They would have no problem making short work of you if they wanted to. If they find you out here all alone in the Serengeti National Park, you will be in big trouble.

You look around. What should you do? You know that normally the thing to do when you get lost is to stay put so others can find you when they come looking, but the hyenas make that impossible.

Off to your right is a large acacia tree that you might be able to climb, while on your left is a dried up creek bed.

With the hyenas getting closer you have to move.

You need to make a decision. Do you:

Run over and climb up the large acacia tree? **P3**

Or

Climb down into the dried up creed bed so you are out of view? **P7**

You have decided to run over and climb up the large acacia tree.

The giraffe has moved off to look for more tasty leaves. As you head towards the acacia tree, you keep looking over your shoulder at the pack of hyenas to see if they have spotted you. Luckily, the pack is upwind so their keen noses may have not picked up your scent yet, especially with all the wildebeest and zebra in the area. Still, they are covering the ground faster than you are.

The hyenas are funny looking animals. Unlike dogs, their front legs are slightly longer than their back legs, causing them to slope up towards their head. The members of this pack have light brown bodies with black spots, black faces, and funny rounded ears. If you weren't so afraid of getting eaten by them, you'd stop and take photos.

You are nearly at the tree when one of the hyenas perks up its ears and yips to the others. Suddenly the whole pack is running as fast as they can right at you!

There is no time to waste. You run as fast as you can towards the tree and start looking for a way up. Luckily you can just reach one of the lower branches. You pull yourself up by clamping your legs around the trunk and grabbing every hand hold the tree offers. Once you are up on the first limb, the climbing gets easier.

The hyenas are under the tree now, eagerly yipping to each other. A couple of scrawny looking ones take a run at the tree and jump, snapping at your legs. You pull your legs up, and climb a little higher. They circle the tree and stare up at you with their black beady eyes. You are trapped.

You take off your daypack and slip out your camera. No point in missing a great photo opportunity just because you're in a spot of danger. After taking a couple shots you pull out your water bottle and have a little sip. You don't want to drink too much because you are not sure when you'll find more. The grasses on the savannah are turning brown, so you doubt there has been much rain recently. You can see down into the creek from here and it looks bone dry.

Some of the hyenas lay down in the shade of the tree. Their tongues hang out of their mouths. Are they going to wait you out? Do they think you will fall?

You remember reading that hyenas hunt mainly at night. Are they going to hang around in the shade until sundown? How will your family find you if you have to stay up here?

You could be in for a long wait and try to make yourself comfortable. After wedging your backside in between two branches and hooking your elbow around another, you start to think about what to do to get out of this situation.

It is pretty obvious that climbing down and running for it would be a really bad idea. The pack of hyena would have you for lunch before you could get five steps. Maybe when they realize they can't get to you, the pack will move on. Or maybe they will see something that is more likely to provide them with an easy meal.

Just as you are about to lose hope, you see a dust cloud in the distance. It is getting bigger. Is the dust cloud being caused by animals or is it the Land Rover coming back for you?

You stand up and look through the leaves and shimmering haze rising from the grassy plain. Further out on the savannah thousands of wildebeest are on the move.

Surely the cloud is moving too fast to be animals. Then you see the black and white Land Rover owned by the safari tour company. But will they see you? The track is quite some distance away from the tree you are in. You didn't realize you'd come so far.

You scold yourself for not leaving something in the road to mark your position. You yell and wave and wish you'd worn bright clothing so the others could see you through the spindly leaves, but the Land Rover isn't stopping. It drives right past your position and races off in the other direction.

"Come back!" you yell.

You sit down again and think. What can you do? It looks like you are on your own, for now at least.

Then you remember the sandwiches in your daypack. Maybe the hyenas would leave you alone if you gave them some food? But then what happens if they don't leave and you're stuck up the tree for a long time and get hungry?

A pair of vultures land in the bleached branches of a dead

tree not far away. Do they know something you don't?

It is time to make a decision. Do you:

Throw the hyenas your sandwiches and hope they will eat them and leave? **P12**

Or

Keep your food for later and prepare for a long wait? **P16**

You have decided to climb down into the dry creek.

You slide in the loose dust and pebbles as you climb down into the dry creek bed. Hopefully you'll be less visible to predators down here. When you reach the bottom, you turn to the north and walk in the direction of the last village your tour passed through.

Unfortunately the creek bed does not run straight and after a few twists and turns, you are not that sure which direction you are heading. You don't want to stick your head up above the top of the bank any more than necessary, just in case some hungry animal spots you and decides you would make a tasty lunch.

Then you remember a trick taught to you by your scout leader. You can use your watch as a compass. First you draw a clock face on the ground with the 12 o'clock position pointing towards the horizon nearest sun. Then you imagine an arrow running out to the horizon between the hour hand, which at the moment is on the two, and the 12 o'clock position. Because you are in the southern hemisphere, this imaginary arrow, which points towards one o'clock, should show you where north is. If you were in the northern hemisphere it would be the opposite and point south. You know this method is not exact, but it's better than nothing.

Using this method, you calculate you are still heading in the roughly the right direction.

In a couple of spots along the bottom of the creek bed,

the mud looks damp, but there is no running water. You know drinking plenty of water is essential in a hot climate so finding some is important if you are going to survive.

As the creek has dried up, deep cracks have formed in the ground, turning the creek bed into a crazy paving of dried mud. Insects buzz and the hot sun beats down on you. You pull your water bottle out of your daypack and have a small sip. You would like to drink more, but until you find another source of water, you want to make sure what you have will last as long as possible.

Lots of acacia trees grow along the creek. Along the branch of one tree sit ten or so brightly colored birds. They are cute little things with light green bodies, yellow chests, orange faces and red beaks. The whites around their beady black eyes give them a slightly startled look. You think they might be Fischer's Love Birds, but you've left your bird identification book on the seat of the Land Rover.

You pull out your camera and take a snap. No point in letting these opportunities go by. You want to document your adventure so that when you get back you'll have lots of pictures to show your family.

After walking for half an hour or so, you figure it's safe to climb up the bank and have a peek at the savannah. When you peer over its rim, you see a plain full of animals. Mainly wildebeest and zebra, but you also see a number of elephants, giraffes, impalas and gazelles grazing on the long grass and spindly shrubs. You are pleased to see that there don't seem to be any leopards or lions, although you know big cats are likely to be lurking nearby as they are known to follow the herd's migration.

From up on top of the bank you can see what look like people moving around the base of a tree further along the creek. With all the dust kicked up by the animals, it's hard to see through the shimmering heat haze, but you hope like crazy that whoever it is can help you contact your family.

You pick up the pace, hoping to get to them before they move off. Five minutes later you can see them much more clearly. What looked like people from a distance, turn out not to be humans at all. Instead it is a troupe of baboons foraging for food. You are not sure you want to get too closed to the baboons because, as with any wild animal, they are unpredictable and can be dangerous if they are frightened or feel threatened.

You are about to sneak around the troupe when one of the females, carrying a small youngster on her back, screeches an alarm.

The others in the troupe immediately start climbing into the branches of the nearest tree. You wonder what it is that has startled them. You don't think they are screeching at you because the noisiest baboons are looking and pointing the other way. Maybe there is a predator nearby. Should you head for the trees too?

Then you see the hyena pack again. Are these the same ones you saw earlier or are they another one?

You sprint for the nearest tree and climb up as fast as you can. Unfortunately, it's not a big tree, and a young baboon has had the same idea.

The hyenas are right behind the young baboon as it runs for the tree. A mother baboon screeches from nearby. Without thinking you lean down and hold out your hand. The young baboon sees your offer of help and grabs on to your wrist.

Just as a hungry hyena leaps up towards the young baboon's legs, you pull with all your strength and hoist the baboon out of harm's way.

You and the baboon sit side by side and look down at the drooling pack. The young baboon is shaking with fear. You don't think it is used to being separated from its mother. Then to your amazement, the young animal slides closer and wraps one arm around your waist. As it snuggles into your side you can feel its heart beating wildly against you.

The baboons in the other trees are making a racket, screeching and hooting at the pack. They raise their fists and bare sharp teeth at the intruders. One baboon watches you intently. Is this the young baboon's mother?

In one of the trees a baboon is breaking off branches and throwing them down at the pack circling below. You are surprised at his accuracy.

It doesn't take long before the members of the hyena pack decide they are not likely to find anything to eat here and move off towards the migrating herds. As soon as they are gone, the baboons climb down from the trees and start looking for insects and grubs again.

The young baboon sitting next to you relaxes and starts picking through your hair looking for nits. You've seen other monkeys do this in documentaries and know that grooming is how the animals bond with each other. It feels funny to have a wild animal picking through your hair but it's not unpleasant.

After grooming you for a few minutes, the young animal climbs down and joins the others in their search for food. The baboon troupe seems relaxed. They obviously don't see you as an enemy.

Now that the threat of the hyenas has passed it is time for you to make another decision. Do you:

Keep following the creek in the hope of finding the village? **P27**

Or

Stick with the baboon troupe for protection? **P31**

You have decided to throw the hyenas your sandwiches and hope they will eat them and leave.

You've been in the tree for over an hour now and the Land Rover hasn't come back. Why aren't your family looking for you? Where have they gone? Are they just going to leave you here on the savannah amongst all the wild animals? They must have driven quite a distance before they noticed you were missing, otherwise they would have found you by now.

The hyenas are lying in the shade of the tree, tongues hanging out of their mouths. Occasionally one will make a funny 'eu eu eu' noise like it is trying to imitate a chimpanzee. Could these be the laughing hyenas you've heard about? The noise they make does sound a bit like someone chuckling under their breath.

Occasionally one hyena will snarl at another. Are they grumpy because they are hungry? Most of the animals are a bit scrawny with ribs showing through their patchy fur.

You reach into your daypack and pull out the two sandwiches you packed earlier. One is ham and cheese and the other peanut butter.

You take the peanut butter sandwich and peel the two slices of bread apart. Then you take the top piece of bread and fling it like a Frisbee as far from the tree as you can. One of the smaller hyenas wanders over to investigate and then gobbles it up. The other hyenas stand up and look up at you. The next piece of bread is the one with all the peanut butter on it. You fling it in the middle of the pack.

A large female snarls and makes a move towards the bread but is beaten to the morsel by a quickly moving male. The female, in a sudden frenzy at missing out on the food, nips at his rear leg. The male yelps and drops the bread and she snaps it up.

You figure the female must be the pack's leader. She is certainly the biggest animal and you remember reading that the females are often the leaders when it comes to hyenas.

You are not sure if feeding the pack will make them want to move on or not, but you figure you've got nothing to lose but your lunch. You break the last sandwich into pieces and line them up along your thigh. You throw one of the pieces to the left and another to the right. Hyenas scatter chasing the scraps. Then you do it again with two more pieces, one left and another right. Again the pack argues over the morsels.

By now the hyena that have missed out on their share of the sandwich are snapping at those that didn't. When you throw the last piece out towards the big female she swallows it whole before the others can get to it.

Seeing how hungry the hyenas are makes you wonder what they would have done to you if you hadn't been able to climb up the tree. It isn't a pleasant thought.

You always knew that life on the African savannah was tough, and that it was a survival of the fittest sort of place. You just never thought you would have a ring side seat for the show.

You lean back against a limb and wait to see what the pack will do now. Not far in the distance, a large herd of wildebeest are getting closer. The wildebeest make a grunting noise that sounds a bit like a cow crossed with a pig. Many of the animals have young with them.

The young wildebeest have long legs for their bodies. Some of them are prancing around, playing, like young animals do. But little do the young wildebeest realize the danger they are in. You have spotted movement in the long grass on the edge of the herd. The lions are nearly the same color as the light brown grass, and they are moving very slowly towards the grazing animals.

When one of the lions breaks cover and rushes at a young wildebeest, the rest of the herd runs off in a wild panic. The animals raise a huge cloud of dust as they run from the lions. You can hear the thump of beating hooves even though they are quite some distance away.

The lions have missed out this time. But no doubt they will try again soon. They stalk after the wildebeest herd.

Hyenas, like dogs, have sharp hearing. It doesn't take the pack long to realize that there may be a meal to be had scavenging around after the lions. The lead female raises her head as if she's smelled lunch, and gets to her feet. Then with a yip to the others, she trots off in the direction of the herd.

Even as you lose sight of the wildebeest that the lions are

following, hundreds more appear in the distance. Zebra and gazelles are also on the move towards the greener pastures in the north.

Before long the hyenas are nothing but tiny brown specks as they run off after the lions. The two vultures have flown off too. They've gone to join the twenty or so other birds circling up high in the thermals created by the hot air rising off the savannah, waiting for the lions to make their kill so they can eat.

After watching the lions and hyenas move further and further away for half an hour or so, you can no longer see any predators on the savannah. All that remain are a family of giraffe munching on the leaves of a nearby tree and a small herd of zebra trotting to catch up with the others.

It is hot, and your water is getting low, if only you could find a village.

It is time for you to make a decision. Do you:

Climb down from the tree and head back towards the road? **P19**

Or

Climb down into the creek bed? **P7**

You have decided to keep your food for later and prepare for a long wait.

You have decided to hang on to your food. Surely the hyenas won't stay under the tree forever. You lean back against a limb and try to relax.

Off in the distance you see more wildebeest moving in your direction. Maybe the hyena will go off and try to catch one of them and leave you alone. You certainly hope so. At least you've got some shade, a little food and what is left of your bottle of water.

Some of the hyenas are skinny. You can see ribs poking out through their fur. It must be a tough life for the animals out on the savannah scrounging for scraps or trying to bring down much larger animals. A serious injury would mean certain death in this unforgiving environment.

After waiting an hour or so, with no sign of the hyenas moving on, you start to get hungry. You take your sandwiches out of your backpack and decide to eat just one. The other you will keep for later.

The hyena's noses twitch as they watch you bite into the cheese sandwich. They lick their lips and make that funny laughing sound again.

The biggest female in the pack stares at you like you are nothing more than a tasty chunk of meat. Her stare makes you a little nervous even though you are well out of her reach.

After you finish the sandwich you take a small sip of water. The bottle is getting low. Only about a third of it remains. You remind yourself not to get greedy. It might be a long time before you have a chance for a refill.

It's not long before you are starting to nod off. Maybe it's the heat, maybe it's because you have just had something to eat. In either case, you know that falling asleep could be fatal. If you fall out of the tree the hyenas will pounce.

You change position and try to wedge yourself into a place where you can't fall, but it's no use. You are going to have to stay awake for as long as it takes the hyenas to go.

As you sit in the tree, you wonder what your family are up to. Are they still looking for you? Why hasn't the Land Rover come back?

Finally the hyena pack gives up on you. The lead female stands and yips to the others and then trots off towards a group of pointy-horned eland grazing in the distance.

Once the hyenas are far enough away, it will be safe to climb down and start looking for a way to get back to the lodge and your family.

You have just started to climb down when you hear the steady whump, whump, whump of a helicopter. It must be someone looking for you!

You make your way down the tree as quickly as you can, but the helicopter is moving fast. By the time your feet hit the ground they have passed overhead and are heading towards the horizon. You run out into the open and wave your arms, but it is too late. The search party is gone.

Will they come back for another sweep? Was it really a search party? Maybe it was just another group of tourists looking at the animals.

Discouraged, you look around and wonder what to do.

It is time for you make a decision. Do you:

Head back to the road and try to walk back to the last village the tour passed through? **P19**

Or

Climb down into the dry creek bed where you will be less visible to predators? **P7**

You have decided to climb down from the tree and head back towards the road.

After sitting in the tree for so long your legs are a bit stiff. You have decided that getting back to the road is a good idea in case the Land Rover or another vehicle comes past, but the idea of walking across open grassland makes you a little nervous. What happens if another predator comes along while you are out in the open?

There are a pile of broken branches by the base of the tree, so you grab one to use as a weapon and start walking. After a few minutes, you turn and look back at the line of acacia trees that run along the dry creek bed and wonder if you are making a mistake.

The dirt road is really little more than two narrow ruts running through the grassland like railway tracks of dried earth.

You rest the branch on your shoulder and start walking back towards the last village your tour passed through. As you walk you try to calculate how far it is. The Land Rover was only travelling slowly, and with all the frequent stops for photographs you figure it is between five and six miles. That's about two hours walking. That's not so bad you think.

But then, when you think of it another way, it is two hours of being exposed in the open, and when you put it like that, it doesn't sound very good at all.

As you make your way along the dirt road, you continually look around. You are also keenly aware of where the nearest tree is. At times you are quite some distance from a climbable tree. It's then that you keep the sharpest look out for suspicious movements in the grass. You want to see potential danger before it sees you. The grass is only knee high, but you are pretty sure if you drop to the ground and lie still you will be hidden from view. Unfortunately, that works for predators too. Especially the lions, as they and the drier patches of grass are similar in color.

Grazing animals are on the move on the grassland all around you. Most seem to be heading in the same direction as you, towards Tanzania's northern border with Kenya. A large group of eland, a type of antelope, is off to your left. Their sharp horns look like they'd be good protection. You figure if the grazing animals are relaxed there probably aren't large predators nearby. If there were, the animals would be nervous.

After walking for nearly an hour you hear a strange sound behind you. You immediately drop flat onto your belly. You can feel your heart beating like crazy. You tilt your head and try to figure out what the noise is. Then you hear it again. It sounds like human voices.

Could it be a search party out looking for you? You slowly rise up on your hands and knees and poke your head above grass level.

A group of young Maasai are trotting along the track in

your direction. The young men wear red robes and each carries a long spear and patterned shield. A couple of the men have brown head pieces covered with brightly colored beads. They move with grace and efficiency and cover the distance between you remarkably fast.

You've never been so pleased to see people in your life. You stand full height and walk slowly towards them, grinning from ear to ear.

The young Maasai are surprised to see you out here on your own. One asks you a question, but you can't understand what he is saying and shrug your shoulders. Then you try to ask them if they are going to the village, but unfortunately they don't speak English any better than you speak their native tongue, Maa. You decide to try sign language.

After waving your arms and making gestures you are pretty sure they understand that you'd like to come with them. One member of the group nods to you and they move off again. You trot along behind them, but keeping up isn't that easy. These young men have longer legs than you do and they are used to the heat and to travelling long distances across the savannah at a pace that is more run than walk.

Just as you think they are about to leave you behind, they stop. Once you've caught up they point towards a low range of hills to the west and then at their spears.

Are they going hunting that way? Are they asking if you want to come with them? Isn't it better for you to stick to the track if you are going to get to the village?

You point at your chest and then point down the track and make a walking movement with your fingers trying to make them understand that you want to go in that direction. They point off to the hills again and smile. You repeat your gestures, but you're not getting through to them.

One of the men has a talk with the others. He points at the tree branch you are carrying and has a chuckle. Then he takes a spare spear he has looped over his shoulder and holds it out to you with two hands like some kind of offering, bowing his head as he does so.

You hesitate, not knowing quite what to do. Giving you his spare spear seems such a generous gesture. You point to your chest and then the spear, trying to ask him in sign language if he is really giving the spear to you. He seems to understand. Again he bows and holds out the spear.

The spear is a much better weapon than a piece of tree branch. Its tip looks sharp and deadly. If these men are about to take off and leave you behind, you'd be silly not to take it.

You reach into your bag and pull out the pocket knife you were given on your last birthday. You hold it up and open the blade. When fully open the blade locks into place. Then you show the man how you push a button on the side of the handle so you can fold the blade away. You hold the knife out on the palm of one hand, as you take hold of the shaft of his spear with the other.

The man smiles and picks up the pocket knife. He opens the blade again. The others crowd around as he runs his finger lightly along the edge of the blade testing its sharpness. He makes excited comments you can't understand to his friends, but from all the smiles you are pretty sure he thinks he's got the best of the trade.

After completing his examination, the Maasai smiles at you once more, folds the blade away and tucks it into his robe. He points down the road, makes walking motions with his fingers and nods to you, as if to confirm that it is the right way for you to walk. Then after a quick word with the rest of the group, the men take off at a trot across the savannah.

You adjust the straps of your daypack and continue on your way, feeling a little better now that you have a proper weapon. The spear has a heavy wooden shaft with a blade on one end. The blade starts out narrow, then widens out to about the same width as your hand, and then narrows into a point again, much like a large gum leaf. You can just imagine the damage it would do to an animal if thrown with any force.

You remember reading that young Maasai have a rite of passage into adulthood that includes hunting for lion. You wonder if you've just witnessed a lion hunting party.

You look at your spear and try to imagine taking a big cat on with it. 'No thank you,' you mumble under your breath. 'Give me a tree to climb any day.'

The sun is getting lower in the sky and you still have quite a distance to cover. You try to imitate the gait of the Maasai men, but you don't have the stamina. In the end you settle for a quick walk.

It is nearly an hour before you see a stockade in the distance. Stout poles, sharpened on one end, are joined together to form a boundary fence. Behind the fence you see the cone shaped roofs of Maasai huts.

A group of smiling children come running out a gate in the fence and gather around you. Their eyes are wide with curiosity. Are they wondering why you are out in the Serengeti all alone?

They look a happy lot dressed in their bright patterned robes of orange and red. If you'd been in Scotland you could have made a half decent kilt with some of the patterned fabric on show.

With a big grin on his face, one of the boys takes your hand and pulls you toward the gate. The other children crowd around and you all move as a group into the village compound.

The Maasai huts are thatched with bundles of grass. Women sit about outside doing various tasks while the younger children play games with pebbles and sticks.

An older man sees you come into the village and walks over. 'Welcome to our village,' he says.

"Great! You speak English. Do you have a phone?" you ask, before realizing what a stupid question it is. You are out in the middle of nowhere. This village doesn't even have electricity.

"Yes. Welcome to our village," the man says once more.

"Do you know any other English?" you ask.

He grins and nods. "Yes English! Welcome to our village!"

A village girl wearing a traditional red dress and bright beads hands you a wooden bowl filled with milk. She looks about 13 years old.

"Those are all the words my grandfather knows. He learned them so he could greet the tourists that come here sometimes. I learned a little English from the missionaries. My name is Abebi. Drink, you must be thirsty."

You introduce yourself and then thank Abebi for the milk before taking the bowl and downing it in one go. You wipe the milk moustache off your upper lip and nod in appreciation before handing the bowl back. "Do you know how far it is to Habari Lodge?"

"About three hours walk," Abebi replies. "But you need to know which tracks to take. There are many that crisscross this area."

"Do many tours come through here? Mine left me behind by mistake. I need to get back to the lodge where my family is staying."

"Not many tourists come to this village these days. They usually go further north along the river to follow the herds and the big cats. They might come once a week, sometimes less."

Now what are you going to do? The villagers are very friendly and the village is probably a safe place to stay, but you don't want to wait a week before another tour comes through.

You are sure your family is looking for you, but you've come quite a distance from where you were left behind. Will they even think to look here?

If it takes three hours to walk to the lodge, you might just make it before dark but you can't be sure.

It is time to make a decision. Do you:

Ask to stay in the Maasai village until morning? **P43**

Or

Keep going along the track and try to get back to the lodge where your family is staying? **P48**

You have decided to follow the dry creek in the hope of finding a village.

The young baboon you shared the branch with is digging into a rotten log looking for grubs. Like the others, she is so intent on finding food that she doesn't notice as you walk off.

You stay near the creek bed where there are more trees. Having something to climb in case of emergency seems a good survival plan. If you take off across the plain, it would be too easy for one of the predators that live here to chase you down.

Hopefully the lions and leopards are more interested in following the herds and catching big juicy wildebeest than they are in eating you. You'll just have to keep your eyes peeled and make sure you stay away from the edges of the herd where the cats lurk waiting to strike.

As you walk, you think about what you should do if you come across a lion. Maybe a weapon of some sort would be a good idea. You look around for a branch you can use as a spear, something with a sharp point would be best.

You also keep an eye out for snakes. Being cold blooded, snakes will often lie on patches of bare ground where they can soak up the warmth of the sun. You've read that there are cobras and puff adders in this area, both of which are extremely venomous. Also large pythons that kill by wrapping their bodies around their prey are common in this part of the Serengeti National Park.

A bit further along you come across a tree that looks like it has been ripped apart by elephants in their efforts to reach the leaves near the top. A couple of branches are lying on the ground at its base. One in particular looks about the right length to make a spear with.

You remember the pocket knife in your pack. Maybe you could lash the knife to the end of the branch. Then you'd have a proper spear.

You find a shady spot, sit on the ground and open up your bag. The pocket knife is one you got for your last birthday and has a long thin blade that locks open. But what can you attach it to the branch with? It will need to be strong if it's going to work as a spear.

There may be something you could use in your daypack, so you tip the contents out on the ground and see what you've got. The only thing you see that might work is the leather strap for your camera. But the strap is too wide to use for binding.

You set about cutting the strap into two thinner pieces with your knife. Then you carve a small notch in the end of the branch to fit the knife's handle. You remember that leather stretches when wet and shrinks when dry, so you pop both strips into your water bottle for a five minute soak.

Once the leather has soaked you can stretch it out and bind it quite tightly around the handle of the knife and the branch. After the second strip of leather has been wrapped around the branch, the blade feels pretty secure.

In the African heat the wet leather doesn't take long to dry. As it does so, it shrinks and tightens around the knife's handle.

You test your spear a couple of times by jabbing it at the mangled tree trunk. It works perfectly. The point of the knife sticks quite a way into the wood without coming loose from the shaft of your homemade spear. You feel a little safer now that you've got a proper weapon, but even with the spear you still plan on climbing up the nearest tree if you see a predator.

But wait. Can't big cats climb trees too? And even if you wanted to, how are you going to climb with a spear in one hand?

You scratch your head and think.

After a bit of thought, you rip off the bottom couple of inches of your t-shirt and use the fabric to make a shoulder strap for your spear. This way you will have a way to carry the spear and keep your hands free for climbing.

Once the strap is tied onto the shaft of the spear, you test your theory by looping the strap over your shoulder and hoisting yourself up into the lower branches of the nearest tree. With the spear resting along your back, the climb is easy. Once you're wedged into the branches you take the spear and point the sharp end downwards. Now if anything tries to climb up after you, you can give it a sharp poke. But will that be enough to fend off a lion or a leopard?

Hopefully you won't have to find out.

After climbing back down to the ground, you start walking again. You know you've got a lot of ground to cover if you are going to get to the village before the sun sets. Dusk on the savannah is the start of hunting time for some predators. You certainly don't want to spend the night out here all alone.

As you walk along the creek you keep a lookout for potential threats. When you come around a slight bend, you see a shallow pond. The water in the pond looks a bit stagnant. The pond's edges are covered in green slime and its surface is alive with insects.

You think about filling your bottle, but then you're not really sure how safe the water is to drink. There are animal droppings and hoof prints everywhere.

You look at your water bottle and see that it is only one third full. You know that will only last you a short while. You are thirsty.

It is time for you to make a decision. Do you:

Fill your water bottle from the pool and have a big drink before moving off? **P38**

Or

Don't fill your water bottle, and keep walking towards the village? **P40**

You have decided to stick with the baboon troupe.

Sticking with the baboon troupe seems a good idea. The troupe posts lookouts while other members forage for food. They seem much better at spotting danger than you are. After all, you never saw the hyenas coming. If it weren't for the baboon troupe raising the alarm you would probably be hyena food by now.

The young baboon you shared the tree with is sticking close to his mother as she strips the bark off a rotten log looking for grubs. Other baboons are picking the seed pods off the various grasses that cover much of the Serengeti.

As the troupe searches for food, its members make their way along the bank of the creek. They may not move fast, but at least they are going in the right direction.

You are startled when the mother baboon moves quickly towards you. You've seen how sharp baboon teeth are, so you hope she's going to be friendly. When she is only a couple of steps away, she holds out her hand. A big fat grub is wriggling between her fingers.

She is offering it to you. You've heard of people eating grubs, but you've never tried one. Would she be offended if you didn't take her offering? What would the grub taste like?

If you are going to be accepted by the troupe, you'd better get used to eating the food they eat. Baboons are reasonably close relatives to humans and you're pretty sure that you could eat most of the things they do without getting sick.

You reach out and pluck the grub from the mother's hand. 'Thank you,' you say, hoping that she will understand the friendly tone of your voice. Then, holding the grub by the head you pop it between your lips and bite down, leaving only the head between your fingers.

"Yum peanut butter," you say as the taste explodes in your mouth.

The mother tilts her head at your words, sees you lick your lips, and seems satisfied that her debt to you for saving her baby has been paid. After making a couple of soft sounds, she moves off to continue her search for food.

There is another log nearby. Using a sharp stick you peel off some bark exposing another big juicy grub.

After a couple of hours, a mature male baboon makes a low whoop and the troop suddenly stops what they are doing and moves off in single file. You wonder what they are doing, but you're happy to tag along. At least you are making progress towards the lodge. You attach yourself near the end of the line. Two young males bring up the rear.

For half an hour or so, the baboons march along the bank of the creek. The youngest of the babies ride on the backs of their mothers. Some of the juveniles play games along the way, jumping on each other's backs and wrestling in the dirt. Occasionally a mother screeches at one of her youngsters when they stray too far from the main group.

The bank on the opposite side of the creek is getting

steeper. Layers of rock within the bank form distinct lines. Many layers are reddish brown in color, but every now and then there is a layer of darker or lighter rock. Is this darker layer compressed plant material? Maybe the light layer is ash from some ancient volcanic eruption.

Finally the troupe stops opposite a crack in the cliff on the far side of the creek. The rocks below the crack glisten with moisture. The troupe descends into the creek bed and then enters the narrow ravine on the other side. Not far up the ravine, you see fresh water trickling into the sand at your feet.

The ravine is cool from being in the shade. A light breeze flows down between the rocks from above. Compared to the heat out on the savannah, this crack in the cliff feels as cool as an air-conditioned room.

When you reach the head of the ravine you see a deep pool formed by the rocks. A steady flow of water seeps out of the cliff face. The baboons gather around the pool and use their hands to scoop the fresh water into their mouths. You do the same. After you've had your fill, you open your daypack and refill your water bottle. Then you take a few pictures of the spring and the baboons with your camera.

Without having pictures as proof, would anyone believe that you were once a member of a troupe of baboons? You somehow doubt it. Half your friends at school didn't even believe you were going to Africa on vacation.

When the baboons have drunk their fill, the troupe leader

heads back down the ravine. Like the others, you follow the leader in single file. Once you get back to the creek bed the troupe once again continues its journey northward.

Before the troupe goes very much further along the creek, you see a flash of light reflecting off something up ahead. You are sure the baboons have seen it too, but they don't seem to be afraid of whatever it is.

Then you see it again. Is the sunlight reflecting off a piece of glass or metal? What would those things be doing way out here on the Serengeti anyway?

The troupe keeps walking. As you near the spot where the reflection was, you see movement. Then you spot a tent set up on an area of flat land not far from the creek. What is a tent doing way out here? Then you remember ... a tent means people!

When a man holding a movie camera stands up from behind a bush, you catch your breath. Then a woman stands up next to him with a fuzzy looking thing on the end of a pole. It must be a microphone.

"What are you doing here with our baboons?" the man with the camera says.

"Your baboons?" you ask. "How are they your baboons?"

The baboons ignore your conversation with the two people and continue moving towards a large acacia tree. The tree has big branches that stretch out like arms. The sun is low, and you wonder if this is where the troupe plans to spend the night.

"We're making a TV documentary. These baboons come to drink at the spring every evening and then sleep in that acacia tree over there. We have been filming animals in this area for two months. Why are you here?"

After explaining about the hyenas and how you came to be travelling with the troupe, the couple invites you into their camp. You're not sure if they believe your story. You must admit it does seem a little unlikely.

When you walk into their camp, a Maasai man is stirring a pot over a fire.

"This is Koinet. He is our guide and cook."

"Would you like something to eat?" the cook asks. "You must be starving if you've been walking all day."

"I'm not too hungry. I've been eating grubs with the troupe. Did you know they taste like peanut butter?"

Koinet nods and smiles.

The white man looks at you like you are nuts. "Koinet, give our young guest a bowl of your stew." Then he turns to you. "I'm sure you will find it far tastier than grubs."

You're not sure if it will be. Peanut butter is one of your favorite flavors, but you eat the stew anyway. It's not bad for something so meaty. When you finish it you have a sip of water from your bottle and then turn to the film makers. "Can you help me get back to Habari Lodge? My family will be worried if I don't turn up soon."

"Habari Lodge? I'm not sure where that is. But did you know that habari means hello in Swahili?"

"That's all very interesting, but how am I meant to get back to my family?"

"I know Habari Lodge," Koinet says. "The only track from here goes around those hills and across the river. It's about two hour's drive."

"Could Koinet take me to the lodge?" you ask. "I would be very grateful.'

The man scratches his head. "I suppose he could, but not until late tomorrow afternoon. We need him for the balloon pick-up in the morning."

"Balloon?"

"Yes Marie and I have a hot air balloon." He nods toward a big cane basket and a bundle of canvas sitting on the far side of the camp next some other equipment. "Tomorrow we'll take it up and fly silently over the herds to the west. The filming should be spectacular. Koinet will track us in the Land Rover and pick us up when we land."

The woman smiles at you. "It is too late to go tonight anyway. You can sleep in the back of the Land Rover. Then tomorrow you can fly in the balloon with Pierre and I or, if you prefer, you can ride in the Land Rover with Koinet. After the flight Koinet can give you a ride to the lodge."

"Sleep on it," Pierre says. "You can let us know what you decide in the morning."

"Okay I will," you say.

The four of you sit around the fire and watch the sun go down. Sunsets here in the tropics are very short. One moment the sun is up, and then bang it's gone. This is so different from where you live.

As you huddle around the fire, the couple tells you about their lives as documentary film makers. It sounds like an exciting life. Maybe you could do something like that when you get older. You've always loved taking photos.

Before long it is dark and the stars have come out like a garden of lights. You've never seen so many stars.

When you start yawning, Marie finds you a pillow and a blanket and shows you to the Land Rover. The back seat is just long enough for you to stretch out on. Before long you are dreaming of life with the baboons.

In the morning you wake up to the sounds of movement. Pierre is fiddling with some equipment on a patch of flat land just beyond the edge of the camp.

Koinet sees you looking out the Land Rover window and waves.

You open the door and walk over to the fire where Marie sits drinking coffee. Koinet is cooking breakfast. Sausages and eggs sizzle in a big frying pan. They smell wonderful.

"So," Marie says from her seat by the fire. "Are you riding or flying today?"

It is time for you to make a decision. Do you:

Go flying in the balloon with Marie and Pierre? **P78**

Or

Ride in the Land Rover with Koinet? **P85**

You have decided to fill your water bottle from the pool.

The water looks a bit dirty but you're thirsty and it is the only water you have found since you were left behind. You use your hand and sweep the insects off the surface and then lower your bottle into the water. The water that fills your bottle has bits of plant material and other things floating around in it but at least it is wet.

You have a couple sips to try it out. It doesn't taste quite as bad as it looks. After drinking your fill you top up the bottle again and put it in your daypack before slinging your spear back over your shoulder and moving off.

You climb the creek bank and have a look around to get your bearings. You decide to leave the creek bed and head north, hoping to reach the village before it gets dark. The winding creek is making your journey much longer than it would be if you were walking in a direct line.

You walk across the savannah quickly, scanning the terrain as you go. Off in the distance you see a large group of antelope grazing. Thankfully no predators are in sight.

Walking is easier now that you've left the uneven ground of the creek bed, but it is hot, and you are thirsty.

Sweat drips down your forehead and back. The more you drink, the thirstier you get. Your mouth stays dry no matter how much water you have. Before you know it your bottle is almost empty.

You don't feel very well. Your stomach hurts and your vision is getting blurry. The next thing you know, your hands are on your knees and you are throwing up into the dust.

The water must have been contaminated. Now you are wishing you'd never had any to drink.

As you throw up again you drop to one knee. You have never felt so sick in your life. By the time you finish throwing up your forehead is burning with fever. You curl up in a ball on the ground to try to make the pain in your stomach go away.

You are getting dizzy and feel like you are about to faint. Then blackness closes in.

Unfortunately this part of your story is over. You made a bad decision by drinking contaminated water. Hopefully someone will find you before a predator does.

It is time for you to make a decision. Would you like to:

Go back to the very beginning of the story and take another path? **P1**

Or

Go back to your last decision and make a different selection? **P40**

You have decided not to fill your water bottle.

You are thirsty and the water in the pond is tempting, but you know that drinking contaminated water can make a person very sick. All of the animal footprints and droppings so close to the pond might mean that drinking the water here is a bit risky.

You'll just have to make do with what little water you have left until you can come across a cleaner source. Hopefully you'll find some soon. You know that moving water is the best. In a moving stream or river the water is purified by running over rocks and gravel and is a lot safer to drink than water from a still pond like this.

After walking for another hour, you crest a small rise and see the circular stockade of a Maasai village in the shallow valley below. Stout poles, sharpened on one end, have been joined together to form a protective fence. Behind the fence you see the round sloping roofs of the villager's huts. These huts are also arranged in a circle. Inside this circle of huts, another circular fence has been built. This is where the Maasai keep their small animals. A number of goats have already been put away for the night and are eating piles of grass provided by their owners. Off to the left of the main village is another larger pen for their many cattle.

As you approach the village, a group of children dressed in colorful robes come running out and surround you. Their eyes are wide with curiosity. You suspect they want to know why you are out in the Serengeti all alone. With a big smile on his face, one of the boys takes your hand. The other children gather around as you are escorted into the village compound.

The Maasai huts are thatched with bundles of grass. Women sit about outside doing various tasks while the younger children play games nearby.

An old man sees you enter the gate and walks over to greet you. "Welcome to our village." he says.

A village girl wearing a traditional red dress and strings of bright beads is holding a bowl filled with milk. She looks about 13 years old.

"Those are the only words my grandfather knows. He learned them so he could greet the tourists that come here sometimes. I learned a little English from the missionaries. My name is Abebi. Here drink this, you must be thirsty."

You introduce yourself and then thank Abebi for the milk before downing it in one go. You wipe the milk moustache off your upper lip and nod in appreciation before handing the empty bowl back. "Do you know how far it is to Habari Lodge?"

"About two hours walk," Abebi replies. "But you need to know which tracks to take. There are many to choose from in this area."

"Do many tours come by here? Mine left me behind by mistake. I need to get back to the lodge where my family is staying."

"Not many tourists come to our village these days. They usually go further north to follow the herds and the big cats. We might see a tour once a week, but sometimes many days pass without us seeing anyone at all."

Now what are you going to do? The villagers are very friendly and the village is probably a safe place to stay, but you don't want to wait a week before another tour comes through.

You are sure your parents will be frantically looking for you, but you've come quite a distance from where you were left behind. Will they even think to look here?

If it takes two hours to walk to the lodge, you might just make it before dark.

It is time to make a decision. Do you:

Ask if you can stay in the village until morning? **P43**

Or

Keep going along the track and try to get back to the lodge where your family is staying? **P48**

You have decided to ask if you can stay in the Maasai village until morning.

"Do you think I could stay here in your village overnight?" you ask Abebi. "I don't think it's safe for me to be out here alone."

The girl nods. "It is not our custom to turn guests away. I am sure mother will let you stay with us until something can be arranged to get you safely back to the lodge."

"Thank you so much," you say. "I was getting a bit worried out there."

The girl grabs your hand and tugs you gently over to a woman sitting on a mat outside the door of one of the huts.

The circular hut is constructed of tree branches tied together into a framework. Between the large branches, thinner sticks are woven around in layers to form walls. Over these walls is plastered a mixture of mud and straw. In the dry African heat the mud hardens like concrete. To keep out the rain and the hot sun, bundles of grass thatch form a thick protective roof.

Abebi says a few words and the woman looks up at you, smiles and nods in welcome. With a sweep of her hand she directs you inside.

"Come," Abebi says as she leads you into the hut.

It takes a minute for your eyes to adjust to the dim light.

The hut is divided into two sections. The first part is a cooking and living area. Through a small doorway, you see sleeping platforms. It is a simple and efficient use of space.

In the living area is a small fire pit dug into the ground. Over the ashes of a previous fire sits a metal grate to hold pots above the flames. A wooden shelf on the wall holds cooking utensils and containers of maize and other foodstuffs.

"You can sleep here," Abebi says, pointing to a clear space along one wall.

You put down your daypack, open the flap and take out your camera and a chocolate bar. You hand Abebi the chocolate. "Here, I want you to have this."

Abebi's eyes light up. "I have had this once before," she says. "It is wonderful."

Abebi opens the chocolate bar, takes one small square and pops it into her mouth. She closes her eyes and rises up onto her toes as the taste sensation runs through her.

"Ummmm..." When the square is gone, she carefully wraps up the rest of the chocolate and puts it on a small shelf. "I will save the rest to share with my family. Thank you for this wonderful gift."

You are amazed at how something so simple can give such pleasure.

Abebi reaches out and takes your hand once more. "Come. Let me show you around the village."

Abebi leads you back outside and over to the circular fence in the center of the village. Here, tucked away from predators, are the village's goats.

"The goats are allowed to graze during the day, but we put them away at night, otherwise the leopards get them."

You take a few photos of the goats and then one of Abebi with her hut in the background.

"Come, let's watch the sunset," Abebi says, as she walks towards the outer wall that surrounds the village.

Along the inside of the wall a mound of earth has been built. Abebi climbs up the mound so she can see over the wall onto the savannah beyond. You scramble up and join her.

The grassland stretches off into the distance. Acacia trees are silhouetted against the sky. Some of them look like umbrellas with their tall trunks and outstretched branches.

"Look over there," Abebi says, lifting her arm and pointing. "See the cheetahs?"

It takes you a moment to spot them on a slight rise a couple hundred paces from the village. There are three of them lying on the ground. Their dark spots stand out against the lighter fur of their bodies. The cats are long and sleek, with tails that swish back and forth.

These cats are built for speed and unlike the much heavier lions and leopards, can run fast enough in short bursts to catch even the quickest gazelle.

"Do they often come near the village?" you ask Abebi.

"They sometimes steal our goats when other game is scarce. But these cheetahs are well fed. Now that the migration has started, there is plenty of game around."

You take your camera and zoom in on the animals. Their coloring reminds you of a tabby cat. Then you notice two cubs tucked up close to one of the females. About the size of a normal house-cat, these two baby cheetah are so cute you want to go out and cuddle them.

"They've got cubs," you tell Abebi. "Here look on the screen you can see them."

Abebi comes closer as you zoom in on the cubs.

The sun is almost at the horizon when you see an old Land Rover coming towards the village.

"Who is that?" you ask Abebi.

"Oh, that's Dr Nelson. He is working in the gorge two day's walk from here."

"Dr Nelson? Does he run a clinic there?"

"No he's not that sort of doctor. He studies old bones and fossils. He is a ... um ..."

"Oh, you mean he's a paleontologist."

Abebi smiles at you. "Yes that's the word."

The children of the village are already running out towards Dr Nelson's Land Rover. The Doctor pulls up outside the gate and jumps down from the driver's seat. In his hand is a bag of sweets that he starts passing out to the children.

Once the bag is empty, he walks in and addresses Abebi's grandfather in the local dialect. After a brief discussion Dr Nelson turns to you.

"So you're the one everybody's been looking for. I heard

a report on the radio a couple of hours ago when I was in town picking up supplies. Your folks are very worried."

"So was I for a while," you say. "Is there any chance you could give me a ride to Habari Lodge?"

"I can, but first I have to drop off this stuff at my camp. These supplies include antibiotics for one of my assistants whose foot is badly infected."

"Can you radio my family and let them know I'm okay?"

"We are out of range here, but I have a satellite phone at my camp. I'm going to stay here tonight. There have been reports of poachers operating in this area. Travelling at night is too dangerous. We can call the lodge tomorrow once we get to my camp."

You like the sound of the doctor's offer but you are only a couple of hours walk to the Habari Lodge. If you go with the doctor you may not get back to the lodge tomorrow at all.

It is time for you to make a decision. Do you:

Go with Dr Nelson to his camp? **P65**

Or

Walk along the road to the lodge in the morning? **P73**

You have decided to keep going along the track to the lodge.

You tell the village girl, that you are going to try to make it to the lodge before dark so you can see your family.

"It is dangerous for someone to travel alone," Abebi says. "I will talk to my mother. Maybe my older brother and I can guide you to the lodge. Predators are less likely to attack a group, and my brother is a warrior. He is sixteen and has already hunted lion."

The idea of an escort to the lodge is the best news you've had all day.

"That would be great," you say.

Abebi runs over and speaks to a woman with short cropped hair wearing a flowing blue dress, and red and white cape. Strings of white beads hang around her long graceful neck. After a brief discussion with her mother, Abebi enters a nearby hut.

A few minutes later she comes out of the hut with a tall, lean young man. He wears a short length of patterned fabric around his waist and carries a shield and spear. Strings of multicolored beads adorn his muscular chest. Abebi carries a length of fabric and a plastic water container.

"This is my brother Biko. Mother says it is okay for us to guide you to the lodge."

"Hi Biko," you say, giving him a smile. "Thank you so much for agreeing to do this."

Abebi translates what you've said and Biko smiles.

Abebi holds up her water container. "Come let's fill our water bottles before we leave."

Abebi leads you over to a well in the corner of the compound and pumps the handle. She unscrews the lid of her water container and fills it to the brim. As you fill your bottle, Abebi wraps her container in the length of fabric and then ties the two ends of the cloth together. She swings the bundle onto her back and loops the fabric around her forehead like a bandanna.

You can't help thinking that Abebi must have a very strong neck to carry water this way. To test your theory, you interlace your fingers together and place your hands on top of your head. Then you pull down with all your strength. It doesn't matter how hard you pull, you hardly feel any weight on your neck at all. All the pressure is straight down.

Abebi laughs when she sees you looking at her sling and pulling on your head with your hands.

"Before the well was drilled," she says, "the village women use to have to carry water a long way each day. It was very hard work. Most of the village women use a sling like this. Others balance their water containers on top of their heads as they walk. It is too hard on your arms otherwise."

As Biko leads the two of you out of the gate and onto the track towards Habari Lodge he scans the surrounding area for danger. It almost looks like he is watching a game of tennis the way his head swings back and forth.

Not far down the track, Biko has a few words with Abebi.

"Biko says that if we are attacked by a predator, stand back to back with him and hold your spear level with the ground with one end braced against your thigh. It is important that we all stick together in a group. Predators always try to separate one out from the others. He says if we stick together we will be fine."

You are pleased to hear Biko's confidence, but you hope you won't need to put his defense tactics to the test.

Now that you are with others and feeling more relaxed, you have a little more time to enjoy the beauty of your surroundings. On both side of the track, wildebeest, zebra and eland are on the move. The fine dust raised by so many hoofs reflects the light and gives the air a golden quality.

Biko says something and points with his spear off to the left.

You look to where he is pointing and see a tribe of meerkats. They are sitting on their haunches on top of a mound of dirt a hundred paces off the road. The older meerkats are watching for predators as the young ones run and leap about in the dust. They don't seem worried about your group passing by.

You stop and rummage in your backpack for your camera, but after a few photos Biko is moving about restlessly and you know he is keen to get moving again.

You are about an hour into your journey when Biko

stops. He speaks urgently to Abebi.

"A vehicle is coming," she tells you.

"Great. We can flag them down and get a ride back to the lodge," you say.

"Biko says they might be poachers. These are very bad men. It is best to hide until we see who is coming."

You follow Biko and Abebi off the road and into a clump of scrub not far away. Biko gestures you to lay flat on the ground. You and Abebi lay side by side in the long grass while Biko stares through the branches trying to see who is coming.

Biko speaks softly to his sister.

"It is poachers," Abebi whispers to you.

Biko drops to the ground as the vehicle nears.

You lift your head ever so slightly and peek through the stalks of long grass. A flatbed truck carrying a group of men with rifles rumbles along the track leaving a cloud of dust in its wake.

Once the truck has passed you start to rise, but Biko's hand on your shoulder presses you back down. It doesn't take you long to realize why. The truck is slowing down.

You wonder if the men on the truck saw you. Are they coming back?

The truck pulls off the track a couple of hundred paces past your position and you hear one of the men shouting. Even though you can't understand what he is saying, you can tell the man is issuing orders to the others.

Gradually you hear the noisy men move away from you. You lift your head once more and see the poachers fanning out across the savannah. Their backs are to you but you can see they are all wearing camouflage gear and carry weapons over their shoulders.

Biko gets to one knee and watches the men intently. He says something to Abebi. It sounds like Biko is angry.

"Biko says the men are hunting Rhino. He hates them for harming such wonderful animals. There are so few left."

As the poachers move further away from the track, Biko stands in a crouch and says three words to Abebi.

"Biko says we are to wait here."

Then keeping low, he streaks across the ground towards the truck.

"What is he doing?" you ask Abebi a little concerned.

"I don't know, but I hope he doesn't do anything stupid. He is so hot headed sometimes."

It doesn't take Biko long to reach the truck. He takes his spear and sticks its point into the two tires on the near side and the next moment he is sprinting back to your position. He is almost back to you when you see a puff of dust kicks up at Biko's feet and you hear the sound of a shot.

Biko shouts as he pumps his legs even harder.

"Run," Abebi say as she grabs your hand and pulls you to your feet.

By the time you are both up and moving, Biko has streaked past you. He looks like he is heading towards a dense patch of scrub a hundred or so paces away. He waves his arms for the two of you to hurry. There is no need for him to tell you twice. You run after him as fast as you can.

You can hear angry men yelling behind you, but you don't slow down to take a look. You hear a couple more shots. One shot pings off the ground beside Biko. Biko starts zigzagging from side to side as he runs. You and Abebi do the same.

By the time you reach the patch of scrub, you are panting. Biko slows to a quick walk but keeps leading you further into the bushes. As you walk you reach into your pack and take out your water bottle. You take a deep drink and pass the bottle to Abebi. She has been forced to leave her water container behind in the rush to flee the poachers. She sips and passes the bottle to her brother who shakes his head as he pulls some foliage aside for the two of you to pass deeper into the undergrowth.

The ground is climbing as you work your way through this rough bit of country. Biko motions you both to stay as low as possible as you traverse a patch of open ground toward a pair of large boulders bigger than houses. Biko leads the way as he squeezes into the gap between the two boulders and up a steep dirt slope that comes out on top of the big rocks. He lies down on his belly and creeps forward to peer over the edge towards the men following below. You and Abebi follow suit.

You can see the truck on the savannah. A couple of men

stand at the edge of the bush wondering if they should pursue you into it. But then their leader calls them back and you see the men start to take the tires off so they can begin their repairs.

Abebi is talking to her brother. She doesn't seem very happy with the danger he has put you all in.

After a heated discussion Abebi turns to you. "It looks like we have two choices. We can move across country for a little while and then rejoin the road a bit further on. But if the poachers fix their tires they might come back down the road and catch us. Or we can get to Habari Lodge by circling around that range of hills over there. But that means we will need to spend the night somewhere, and won't get to the lodge until tomorrow.

It is time for you to make a decision. Do you:

Try to rejoin the road a bit further on so you get to the lodge today? **P55**

Or

Circle around the hill and get to the lodge tomorrow? **P60**

You have decided to try to rejoin the road a bit further so you can get to the lodge today.

"I really want to try to get back to the lodge today if possible," you tell Abebi. "If the poachers come back, we can just hide in the bushes again."

Abebi has a word with her brother. In the beginning he shakes his head no, but after a little convincing, he shrugs his shoulders and agrees.

"Okay we will try," Abebi says. "But my brother says that we will have to walk without talking so he can listen."

You nod in agreement, realizing the importance of having as much time as possible to hide should the poachers come back.

The three of you stand up and start back down the gap between the two boulders. Once you get into the undergrowth, rather than heading back the way you came, Biko turns to the right and works his way along the side of the hill. You notice that Biko makes sure there is a barrier of trees and scrub between you and the road at all times. Once again he speaks to Abebi.

"Biko wants us to walk quietly in single file so we don't disturb too many animals and give away our position," Abebi tells you.

After walking for fifteen minutes or so, Biko turn down the slope and starts making his way back towards the dirt road. When you finally exit the undergrowth and look back towards where the flatbed truck had stopped, you can only see haze and wildebeest. You figure the poachers must be a couple of miles away by now. Most likely they have resumed their hunt. Why would they bother looking for you when they have rhino to hunt?

You secretly hope the rhinos charge at them and wreck their truck. Or that the rangers catch them and put them in jail.

By the time you've rejoined the road the sun is low in the sky. The horizon has turned red and orange with intense patches of gold and yellow. The trees are now silhouetted against the sky and look like structures you'd see in a science fiction film set on an alien planet.

The sun sets quickly near the equator. As the three of you walk you can see the sky changing, getting darker minute by minute.

Biko's pace seems to have increased and you know why. Getting caught out in the open, at night on the savannah, is just asking for trouble.

Just as the sun drops behind the horizon, you see the lodge in the distance. Like the Maasai village the lodge also has a strong fence built around it perimeter to protect the guests from the many predators that hunt at night.

"There it is!" you say breathing a big sigh of relief.

Biko says something to Abebi as he starts walking even faster.

"Hurry," Abebi says. "Biko has seen movement in the

grass. He thinks it might be lions. Get ready in case we need to protect ourselves."

You cannot believe that you might get eaten within sight of the lodge. You've come so far. The three of you break into a trot.

A roar to your left is so loud you nearly poop your pants. Biko breaks into a run for the lodge. You and Abebi do the same.

You hear movement behind you. Expecting to be dragged down by a pair of gigantic claws at any second you run even harder. Then a man runs out of the gate. He has a rifle in his hands and points it into the air and fires. Bang, bang, bang! The noise is deafening.

"Quickly, into the compound!" he yells and waves his arm.

You don't need to be told twice. The three of you run pass the man. He fires two more shots and turns and rushes through the gate after you, slamming it shut behind him.

"You three youngsters were nearly cat meat," the man says. "What are you doing out here at dusk?"

You explain to the man how you came to be in the company of the two Maasai and how they helped you get back to the lodge after being abandoned on the savannah.

"Oh so you're the one who ran off from the tour."

"I didn't run off!" you say. "The stupid driver left me behind!"

"That's not what he says. He says you deliberately snuck

off. Your family is very disappointed in you."

You can't believe what you are hearing. "But why would I..."

"Never mind, you're safe now. I'd better get onto the radio and let the searchers know you've been found. Your family will be pleased to see you when they get back."

"Get back? Where have they gone?"

"They're out looking for you of course. They've been out all day. Come. Bring your friends. You three must be hungry after your long walk."

This was the first thing the man had said that made any sense. Why would any sane person get off a tour and walk out onto the savannah alone? Was he crazy?

You are just finishing dessert when your family comes into the dining room and rush over to greet you. After a few hugs, and an explanation of how you came to be left behind, you introduce you family to Abebi and Biko.

Your family thanks the two young Maasai for getting you back safe and promise to organize a ride for them back to their village the next morning.

"Thank you," Abebi says. "I've never had a ride in a Land Rover before."

"Oh and we must take lots and lots of chocolate," you say. "The village children love chocolate."

Congratulations you made it back safely to your family. This is the end of this part of your adventure. Have you tried all the possible paths this story takes?

You have a decision to make. Would you like to:

Go back to the very beginning of the story and take another path? **P1**

Or

Go to the list of choices and start reading from somewhere else in the story? **P113**

You have decided to circle around the hills to get to the lodge the following day.

As the three of you watch from above, some of the poachers start work repairing the truck. A man on the back lifts up a cover to reveal two spare tires and a toolbox. He lifts the tires up and rolls them, one at a time along the deck and over the edge to the ground.

You can see Biko's scowl as he watches the men jack up the truck and undo the nuts that hold the wheels on. He grumbles something to Abebi.

Abebi translates and tells you that if Biko had known the men had more than one spare he would have damaged all of their tires.

You pull your camera out of your daypack and put on the telephoto lens so you can zoom right in on the poachers. Abebi and Biko are keen to move on, but you want to take photos of the poachers. You zoom in on face after face, clicking photo after photo. You also take photos of the men's truck with its distinctive green stripe down the side. Perhaps the photos can help to stop them.

Before long the poachers have replaced the two tires and have driven further onto the savannah. Once again they get off the truck and spread out towards a pair of rhino.

You feel like yelling a warning to the rhino, but you know there would be no chance of them hearing you. And even if they could, the men would hear you as well.

Once you are satisfied with the photos you've taken, you tell Abebi you are ready to go.

Just as the three of you walk back into the bush and turn towards the north, you hear shots in the distance. Each shot makes you wince. You know what the shots mean and it makes you sad that people would kill such magnificent animals just for their horns. You decide some humans are worse than animals. You look towards Abebi. A tear trickles down her face, leaving a line in the fine dust. Biko's jaw is clenched in anger. You grit your teeth. You are glad you took photos so the police have proof of these men's actions. Hopefully they will help bring them to justice.

After walking for another hour, Biko stops next to a large rock. It looks like he has found you a place to stay the night.

Biko and Abebi start collecting firewood. You drop your pack and do the same. Before long you've got a good stack. Biko drags over a couple of bigger logs to throw onto the fire once it is burning well.

Biko builds the fire about three paces out from the face of the rock.

"We will sleep between the fire and the rock," Abebi tells you. "We don't want the fire going out during the night. As long as the fire is burning, the predators will keep away."

You nod and sit on the ground with your back to the rock. The rock face overhangs a little so you don't have to worry about animals sneaking up on you from behind.

The sunsets are brief near the equator. Within half an

hour the sky is full of stars. Being so far from the city lights means you can see the stars of the Milky Way much clearer. You try to imagine how many stars there must be out there. There are more than you could possibly count in a thousand years.

Abebi sits down beside you. "We will take turns sleeping and feeding the fire," she says. "Try to sleep now if you can, Biko will wake you when it is time for you to be on lookout."

You scoop out a shallow hole in the ground for your hip and lie on your side with your back to the rock. You can feel the rock's warmth as it sheds the heat it has absorbed from the sun during the day.

The physical exertion of walking and running has tired you out. It is not long before you start dreaming that you are riding amongst the herds of wildebeest on horseback. It reminds you of the cattle-drives there used to be in the Wild West. Then before you know it, Biko is shaking your shoulder.

The night passes without any problem. At dawn, Biko leads you and Abebi across the grassland in a big arc around the hill.

Within an hour you see a track heading northwards.

"Is that the track to the lodge?" you ask.

Abebi has a word to her brother. Biko nods and says a few words.

"Yes, we are about an hour from the lodge."

Soon you will be reunited with your family. You cannot wait to see the look of relief on their faces when you walk into the compound.

The three of you walk into the compound just as the Land Rovers are loading up for the day's search. Your family is talking to the driver who left you behind. When they see you with Abebi and Biko they shout out in surprise and rush over to hug you.

The driver also seems relieved.

When your family finishes hugging you, you walk over to the driver.

"You owe me an apology," you say. "Why don't you count that everyone is on board before you take off?"

The driver kicks the dirt with his foot. "I'm so sorry. I didn't realize you were out of the vehicle. Is there any way I can make it up to you?"

The driver seems genuinely sorry.

"I owe these two something," you say, turning to Abebi and Biko. "Without them I might not have made it back. They put themselves at risk to help me."

"I will make sure they are well rewarded," the driver says.

While you've been talking to the driver, the lodge manager has wandered over. You explain about the poachers and how you've taken photographs of them.

"We're in luck," the manger says. "Normally poachers leave the area before we have a chance to call the authorities, but because of you getting lost, there are police all over the area. I'll radio them now and let them know you've shown up so they can concentrate on catching the poachers."

Abebi looks ecstatic when she hears this. She explains what the manager has said to Biko

Abebi takes your hand and smiles. "Sometimes good can come from things going wrong. If you hadn't gotten lost today those poachers would never have been caught."

You smile back. "And I wouldn't have made some new friends."

Congratulations, you made it safely back to your family. This part of your adventure is over, but have you found all the possible paths?

It is time to make another decision. Would you like to:

Go back to the very beginning of the story and try another path? **P1**

Or

Go to the table of contents and start reading from another place? **P113**

You have decided to go with Dr Nelson to his camp.

Deciding to go with Dr Nelson is the safe option. You could have tried walking to the lodge, but being out on the savannah alone is not a good idea, especially for someone who isn't familiar with all the possible dangers.

After saying a final goodbye to Abebi and her family you climb into Dr Nelson's Land Rover. The back of the vehicle is filled with boxes. Everything is coated in a fine layer of dust. You wipe your finger along the dashboard amazed at how thick it is.

"You wouldn't believe I gave this vehicle a good clean before I left town. The fine dust seeps in, even with the windows closed. These old Land Rovers are reliable, but they certainly aren't dust proof."

You wave to the children as the two of you drive out of the village. A few of the older boys run along after you. It is nearly a mile before the last of the boys give up and return to village.

At a junction about half an hour out of the village, Dr Nelson turns to the west and heads towards a low range of hills in the distance.

"I've been working in the gorge for nearly ten years," Dr Nelson tells you. "We've uncovered some of the oldest remains of early man ever found."

"Really?" you say, turning towards Dr Nelson. "How old are you talking here?"

Dr Nelson raises his bushy eyebrows a couple of times and smiles. "Two million years or so..."

You must admit you weren't expecting it to be quite that old. You try to imagine how far back that is and how many generations of people that would be.

"And you've been digging for ten years?"

"And writing about my findings. It's incredibly exciting to discover a stone tool used by a person who lived long ago. When I see these tools I know they weren't all that different from us."

"But isn't it lonely working so far from civilization?" you ask. "Don't you ever miss TV?"

"Living here is like watching a reality show. There are always interesting things happening all around you if only you take the time to look. We see so many animals, and have the excitement of our discoveries. Plus I have the research team to keep me company. We have a great time."

You must admit, being here in Tanzania, does make you feel like you are in an episode of Survivor or one of those documentaries on The Discovery Channel.

For a while the two of you are silent, both absorbed in your own thoughts. The track has turned further north and runs along the river. Water levels are low because of the lack of rain, but the river is still deep enough in some spots to make a good bathing place for elephants and hippos. Dr Nelson obligingly slows as you take lots of photographs.

As you near the hills the road starts to climb. When you

turn and look back, you get a fantastic view of the savannah below. It is only from this higher altitude that you get an idea of how many animals are on the move. Herds stretch as far as you can see. This has got to be one of the most incredible sights you have ever seen.

"Still think you need TV out here?" Dr Nelson asks.

"I see what you mean. This is amazing." You lift your camera and take a couple more shots. "I'm going to get one of these pictures blown up and put it on my bedroom wall."

After crossing the river you enter a wide valley. With the gain in altitude, the landscape is changing. Towering cliffs, layered with different colored rock, appear in the distance. The lower layers are pale like sand, but then higher up, the rock face turns almost red.

"Looking at the strata in these cliffs is like looking back in time," Dr Nelson tells you. "Each layer spans a time longer than you can imagine. It is the erosion of these layers that has exposed the fossils and artifacts my team and I are looking for."

The further you go, the narrower the valley becomes. Finally you drive around a corner and spot Dr Nelson's camp set on a level piece of ground above a shallow creek bed. There are two tents. A large awning is tied between some trees to provide extra shade.

"Come and meet the others," Dr Nelson says.

You are not sure why, but you expected the other members of Dr Nelson's team to be old like him. These people are not that much older than yourself.

"Meet Jeremy and Alice. They are university students from California here for the season."

Alice smiles at you and holds out her hand. Jeremy doesn't look too well. He is leaning on a makeshift crutch and his foot is wrapped in bandages.

Dr Nelson sees how pale Jeremy is and goes to the back of the Land Rover to get the medicine. Then he gets Jeremy to sit down and starts to unwrap his dressing.

Jeremy's foot is red and oozing pus. You can smell the infection from where you are standing a few steps away.

"Here take these capsules," Dr Nelson says. "I'm going to wash this and put some antiseptic cream on the wound. You'll need to rest up for a few days and let the antibiotics do their job."

Once Dr Nelson finishes dressing Jeremy's wound, he comes over to where you are sitting. "Well I suppose we'd better phone the lodge and let your parents know you are all right."

"That would be great," you say, smiling at the thought of talking to your family.

It takes a few minutes for the doctor to phone town and get the lodge's number, but then he hands you the phone and you hear a familiar voice.

"We've been so worried!"

"Well I'm safe now, sorry I scared you all," you say.

After a chat with your family, you pass the phone back to

the doctor for a minute. He is talking to the lodge manager.

"The lodge is sending a Land Rover out to pick you up. It will be here in about three hours," the doctor says after hanging up. "In the meantime would you like to have a look around the diggings?"

"Sure," you say, excited to see with your own eyes what doctor Nelson has been telling you about during the drive. "Can I have a go at digging?"

"If you like," he says. "With Jeremy out of action, we could use some extra muscle."

After sandwiches for lunch, Alice and the doctor lead you along a narrow path to a spot where there are piles of earth and a series of trenches. Wooden frames on short legs with screen mesh bottoms sit on the ground. Alice explains what you are looking at.

"We sift the dirt through these frames to make sure we don't miss anything. Even the smallest piece of bone can be important. We've been finding quite a few tools in this area."

Then the doctor points to a bank of earth and rock.

"Most of the interesting stuff is coming out of that bank there. You still interested in doing some digging?"

"Sure, what should I do?"

Dr Nelson hands you a shovel. "Just fill the wheelbarrow with dirt from that bank and wheel it over to where Alice is sifting."

You nod, put the shovel into the wheelbarrow and grab

its handles.

"Slow is good," Dr Nelson tells you. "If you notice any bones, stop digging right away and call one of us. We want to avoid any damage if possible."

It takes you about ten minutes of hard work to fill the wheelbarrow. As you and Alice sift the clumps of dirt through the sieve you spot a teardrop shaped bit of grey rock about five inches long. The rock's edge has small chips on its surface.

"This looks interesting," you say, holding it up for Alice's inspection.

Alice's mouth drops open. "Wow!" she says. "You just found a stone age tool in your very first load. How lucky is that!"

Dr Nelson hears Alice's words and comes over to investigate. He holds the adze in his fist and demonstrates how this rock would have been used for chopping. "See how the edges of the stone have been chipped away to sharpen it? We might have to keep you around as our lucky charm. Alice here didn't find a single thing her first week."

On a trestle-table, set up under a sun shade, all the artifacts and pieces of bone the team has found are laid out in neat rows. Each item has a card tucked beneath it noting when, where and who had found each piece.

Alice takes the tool you found and writes a description of it on an index card with the date and time. She places the adze on the table beside the others and then asks for your details and adds those to the card too before slipping it under your find.

"Well you're part of the team now," she says. "This piece will end up in a museum somewhere and your name will stay with it. How cool is that?"

You find yourself grinning. You have to admit you like the idea of having your name attached to a scientific expedition. It's like being a part of history.

You are keen to get digging again. Time seems to go by fast when you're hunting for artifacts. Each new shovel full of dirt could contain the next big discovery. After half a dozen more wheelbarrow loads, you all go back to check on Jeremy and have a drink.

This is turning into one of your best holidays ever, despite being left behind by the safari.

When you hear the sound of a vehicle coming up the track, everyone rises to their feet. It's the Land Rover from the lodge.

As soon as the vehicle stops, its doors fly open. Your family rushes over to greet you.

"I didn't realize you were all coming to pick me up!" you say, pleased to see them.

"Of course we all came. We wanted to make sure you weren't left behind again!"

Congratulations, you've made it to the end of this part of the story, but have you followed all the possible paths? But have you flown in a balloon, or made friends with the baboons? Seen poachers? Been chased by lions?

It is time to make another decision. Would you like to:

Go back to the very beginning of the story and try a different path? **P1**

Or

Go to the list of choices and start reading from another part of the story? **P113**

You have decided to walk to the lodge in the morning.

After spending the night in the hut with Abebi and her family, you step outside and notice Dr. Nelson getting ready to leave. Abebi has told you there are many tracks in this area and you want to make sure you take the right one. You are hoping that Dr Nelson can draw you a map.

"Are you sure you don't want to come to my camp?" he asks. "It's not safe walking on the savannah alone you know."

"I've made it this far okay," you tell the doctor. "If what you've told me is correct the lodge is only a couple of hours walk from here."

"I'll tell you what," Dr Nelson says. "I'll give you a ride to the next junction. Then at least you'll be on the right track to the lodge."

You accept the doctor's kind offer and after saying goodbye to Abebi and her family, you jump into the passenger seat.

He explains how he'd like to take you all the way, but the supplies he's carrying include antibiotics for one of his crew who has a bad infection. "He might lose his foot if I don't get these antibiotics back to him soon."

You nod and explain to the doctor that you understand and that it's okay. You have your spear for protection. And now that you only have to walk half as far you are sure you will make it without any trouble.

"Lucky for you, most of the big cats are further north following the herds at the moments. Otherwise it would be suicidal to go on foot alone."

After bumping along the narrow track for half an hour or so, you come to a junction.

Dr Nelson points towards two ruts heading towards the northwest. 'That's the one you want. When I get to my camp, I'll phone Habari Lodge and tell them you are on your way. They'll probably send out a Land Rover to pick you up if you haven't made it there already.' Then he grabs an oily red rag from the back seat. 'Here take this. Throw it in the middle of the road if you have to leave it for any reason. Then the Land Rover will know where to start looking.'

You tuck the red rag into you back pocket and hop out of the vehicle. 'Thanks for the lift,' you say before slamming the door.

"Good luck!" the paleontologist yells as he drives off.

You watch as the Land Rover disappears behind a row of tree and all you can see is a dusty cloud heading towards a low range of hills.

Apart from some squawking birds in a nearby tree, it is silent. Once again you are alone on the Serengeti.

After adjusting your backpack you rest your spear over one shoulder and start walking. You can see the herds off in the distance. From where you stand they look like a swarm of ants stretching from one end of the grassland to the other.

You slept well and are feeling refreshed. The morning sun is still low in the sky, but you can already feel the temperature rising. Before long it will be scorching. It is time to pick up the pace before it gets too hot.

As you come over a slight rise, you see a wisp of smoke in the distance. Could this be the lodge? You doubt it somehow. There is no way you have come far enough to be at the lodge already.

Still, smoke usually means people. Maybe it is one of the safaris having a coffee break. Then you see the vultures. Twenty, maybe more, are circling above. Others are on the ground feeding.

You duck down and move off the track. As you creep forward you use the long grass and scrubby bushes as camouflage. If this fire is man-made, where is their vehicle? Would the vultures be on the ground if there were people about? You don't think so.

After scanning the surrounding grassland and seeing no people you slowly stand up for a better look. The camp is deserted. Vehicles and footsteps have flattened the grass in places, but whoever was here has gone.

The carcass of some dead animal lies on the ground twenty or so paces from a smoldering fire pit. As you approach, some of the feeding vultures fly off, only to have their places taken by others. The ugly looking birds stare at you unafraid. Some have pieces of meat hanging from their curved beaks.

You turn your head away. Vultures ripping flesh off the carcass is not a pretty sight.

You are almost back to the road when you hear the sound of flapping wings. The vultures are flying off. They have been frightened by something.

You can see the whole carcass now. It is a rhino, minus its horn. You feel like screaming into the air at the horrible waste of the animal's life. It must be those awful poachers. How can they do this? You shake your head and feel tears forming.

Then you spot what has scared off the vultures. A mother lion and her two cubs have come to investigate.

You move as fast as you can back to the track. Thankfully there is no need for the lioness to chase you when she has an entire rhino to eat. She immediately starts pulling pieces of flesh off the rhino for her young cubs to eat. When you are a safe distance away, you take out your camera and zoom in on the action. After getting a few shots, you move off again. If one lion has been attracted by the vultures, there may be others. You don't see any point in pushing your luck.

Forty five minutes later you are pleased to see the stockade fence of Habari Lodge in the distance. The ground where you stand is slightly higher in elevation than the site where the lodge is. This enables you to see over the barricade into the compound where a number of vehicles are parked up.

This seems a bit odd to you. Why aren't the Land Rovers

out looking for you, or at least out on safari? Why are they parked in the compound at this time of day?

Then you hear shots.

You crouch down behind a small shrub and stare down into the compound. What is going on? Why is someone shooting? Something is definitely wrong.

You reach into your bag and pull out your camera. Using its 10x zoom function you study the compound and try to figure out what is happening. Then you see a group of men dressed in a variety of old army clothes and camouflage gear, pushing the lodge guests into a line along the veranda. The men are carrying rifles. They must be the poacher gang.

One of the men is waving his arms and yelling. Another shoots his gun into the air. You see your family lined up with the other guests.

What are you going to do now? These are violent men with guns.

It is time to make a decision. Do you:

Sneak down to the lodge and try to help your family? **P96**
Or
Go back the Maasai village for help? **P105**

You have decided to go flying in the balloon.

You've always been a little afraid of heights, but how often do you get a chance to fly in a hot air balloon? It is an opportunity too good to pass up. Just imagine the photographs you will be able to take.

Koinet puts two fat sausages and a couple of eggs on a plate and passes it in your direction. You are starving after all your walking yesterday and dig right in.

"Juice?" Koinet asks you.

The orange juice tastes freshly squeezed. It isn't that cold, but the flavor is wonderful.

You catch the woman's eye and nod over towards the man. "What's he doing?"

"Pierre is setting up the fan to fill the balloon."

"Fan?" you ask.

"Yes we have a small generator that runs an electric fan. We lay the balloon out on the ground and hook up the basket. Then, with the mouth of the balloon held open, the fan blows air into it. Once the balloon has partially inflated, the burner is fired up to heat the air inside so the balloon stands up."

"That makes sense," you say.

"Then the burner is fired in short bursts and more and more hot air rises up into the balloon until there is enough lift for us to take off."

"We tie the basket down until everyone is aboard,"

Koinet says with a grin. "Then I chase you in the Land Rover."

"How do you steer?" you ask.

The woman laughs. "You don't really. Sometimes the wind blows from a slightly different direction at different heights, but mainly we just wait until the wind is blowing in the right direction and go with it. Today it is coming from the southeast. This means we will fly towards the northwest, which is the same direction the herds are migrating. Today should be perfect for filming."

You hurry to finish breakfast and then ask if you can help.

"Sure," Pierre says. "Help me unpack the balloon and get it laid out on the ground."

The two of you pull the balloon out of its protective bag and drag it out through the short grass. Cords are then attached from the balloon to points along the top rim of the basket.

"See those hooks along the side of the basket? We will attach bags of sand to those so we can drop them quickly if we need reduce weight and climb quickly."

It does not take long before everything is hooked up, and the fan is blowing air into the gaping mouth of the balloon. Soon, the brightly colored sections of fabric that make up the balloon's panels are billowing in the breeze.

"Hey Marie," Pierre yells to the woman. "Fire up the burner!"

With a roar like a jet engine, a tongue of flame shoots out

from the burner and fires hot air into the balloon. Thirty seconds later, another burst rips through the air.

The balloon is rising. After a few more bursts it is standing up and only a rope tied to a stake in the ground is keeping the balloon from taking off.

"Okay you two, get your stuff and climb aboard," Pierre says.

You grab your camera, check that your water bottle is full and walk towards the basket. Marie has a pack of equipment and Pierre is checking that his movie camera is working.

The three of you climb into the basket, which settles back onto the ground with the extra weight. Pierre pulls the lever and shoots another couple of burst of flame into the balloon.

You feel the basket shift, and then lift slightly. Koinet unties the rope from the stake and wraps it around his wrist. His extra weight keeps the balloon down.

"Ready for take-off," Pierre says to Koinet as he fires another long burst.

Koinet releases the rope and up you go. Another short burst and you are above the acacia trees and climbing.

"Wow," you say as you watch the ground fall away. "This is amazing!"

Marie puts her hand on your shoulder. "See how we are drifting towards those wildebeest in the distance? The idea is to film from just above as we glide silently over them. With a little luck, they won't even know we are there."

You rest your arms on the edge of the basket and look out at the savannah below as you drift with the breeze. You look back towards the camp and are surprised how far you have come already. What is most unexpected is the quiet.

Every now and then Pierre breaks the silence by giving the burner a quick blast to maintain your height, but otherwise it is unbelievably peaceful.

Spread out in front of you are a series of ponds reflecting the early morning light. A narrow band of water connects them together so they look like a necklace. A line of acacia trees follow the course of the river.

As you pass over the first pond you see the grey backs of twenty or so hippo swimming and splashing in the water. A baby hippo sticks close to its mother. A bit further along you see why. Crocodiles are sunning themselves on the river bank.

The silver reflection of the water contrasts with the golden grasses of the savannah as it stretches towards the purple hazed hills at the horizon. Dirt tracks crisscross the landscape. They must be animal highways.

A leafless tree by one of the ponds seems to be covered in black and white flowers, but as you get closer to the tree, the flowers suddenly take off and you realize they are not flowers at all but a flock of storks.

Beyond the river a small gang of buffalo trot northwards. You see a parade of elephants too. One of the elephants has a young one trailing behind.

Ten minutes later, you are silently hovering over thousands of wildebeest, zebra and antelope making their way northward. Pierre starts filming and Marie dangles her microphone on a cord down from the balloon so that it hangs not far above the animals.

Marie looks at you and holds her finger to her lips. "Shhhh..."

The sound of so many animals around you is astounding. Soaring just above the herd makes you feel part of one of the most spectacular migrations on earth. You remember reading that more than one million wildebeest, 200,000 zebra and 400,000 gazelle migrate each season. An uncountable number of them stretch out before you.

You are taking shots as fast as you can push the button on your camera. Off near the edge of the herd you see a pride of lions stalking from the long grass. It looks like the lions are waiting for a chance to isolate one of the wildebeest from the herd.

You have glided over the herd for as long as possible without firing the burner so the balloon is getting quite low.

Pierre puts down his camera and reaches for the lever to ignite the burner, but when he pulls the handle nothing happens. "Marie, please release a sandbag, there is something wrong with the burner."

Marie reaches over the edge of the basket and unhooks one of the sandbags. She lets it drop to the ground below, just missing a zebra. You feel the balloon rise a little, but before long as the air in the balloon continues to cool, you start sinking towards the ground one more.

Pierre is frantically making adjustments to the equipment. "Another sandbag," he says, looking in Marie's direction.

You detect a hint of concern in his voice, but Marie calmly follows his instructions and releases another bag of sand.

"This ignition isn't working," Pierre says. "We need to look for a landing spot."

When you look ahead, along the balloon's flight path, all you can see are animals and a number of large acacia trees.

"I see a landing spot past this row of trees," Pierre says. "But we need to lose some more weight if we are going to make it over them."

Marie releases the last two sandbags and you rise once more. The balloon makes it past the first few trees but as the balloon slowly descends again you realize you are not going to get past the last of them.

"Stay down below the rim of the basket," Marie says. "And hold on, we're going to clip the top of that tree."

You can see she is right. The balloon is sinking fast and you are heading right towards the upper branches of the big acacia.

"Hang on ... here we go!" Pierre yells.

The sound of snapping branches you expected. What you didn't expect was for the basket to tip on its side when it hooked up in the tree. You are no longer sitting in the bottom of the basket but kneeling on its inner wall.

A good sized branch is right in front of you. Maybe if you jumped out of the basket onto the branch, the balloon will lighten and have enough lift to clear the tree. You could save the day.

It is time to make a quick decision. Do you:

Jump out of the balloon onto the branch? **P90**

Or

Stay in the basket? **P92**

You have decided to ride in the Land Rover with Koinet.

"I think I'd rather stay in the Land Rover with Koinet," you tell Marie.

You've decided not to fly in the hot air balloon with a pilot you don't know, despite it sounding like fun. You've never been very good with heights anyway and going up in the balloon sounds scary.

Koinet serves you a breakfast of eggs and sausages. While you eat, Marie drinks her coffee.

"No problem," Marie says. "Koinet will be pleased to have some company for a change."

After eating your breakfast you wander over and help Pierre ready the balloon. He's rigged up a big fan to blow air into the mouth of the balloon. Once it's nearly full Marie fires the burner to heat the air inside.

Slowly the balloon stands up, tethered only by a rope tied to a stake in the ground.

Pierre and Marie load up their gear as you and Koinet hold the balloon steady. When Pierre gives the signal, you both release the balloon and watch it sail up into the sky.

"Quick now," Koinet says. "Into the Land Rover, we don't want them to get away on us."

The next thing you know, you are thundering along a dirt track giving chase.

The balloon looks spectacular. Its multicolored panels

really stand out against the powder blue sky.

Koinet drives like a crazy man to keep up. Unlike the balloon that flies in a straight line, he needs to find a way around different obstacles. When the balloon reaches the river, things get really tricky.

While Koinet looks for a shallow place to cross, the balloon flies on. The first possible crossing spot is surrounded by hippos.

"We can't cross here. Too dangerous," Koinet says. "Did you know that hippos kill more people each year than lions?"

"I remember reading that," you say. "Did you know that more people are killed by cows than sharks each year?"

"Really?" Koinet says. "Just goes to show that any animal can be dangerous if you don't watch out."

The next place Koinet finds to cross the river is wide but shallow. A couple of crocodiles lie on the riverbank in the sun but Koinet manages to drive around them and ease the Land Rover into the water. A small wave surges in front of the vehicle as it pushes its way through the murky river.

On the opposite bank, Koinet points to a flock of black and white storks sitting in a tree. Their call sounds like clacking wood. You get a good shot of them just as they fly off.

Once the two of you are across the river, you speed off across the savannah after the balloon again. There are wildebeest, zebra and gazelle everywhere. Never before have you seen so many animals in one place.

Off in the distance the balloon has come down to cruise just over the herd. You see Marie's microphone dangling from the basket of the balloon.

"We'll stay back a little so the vehicle doesn't disturb the animals," Koinet says.

Just as you are about to ask Koinet a question, he stomps on the brakes.

"Look," he says pointing off to the right. "There in the long grass. Do you see them?"

You squint and try to see through the heat haze and dust. It takes a few moments, but you finally see a lion. Koinet creeps forward in the Land Rover. Then you see two more lions just beyond the first. They are eating a gazelle.

Koinet points up at the sky where the vultures are circling. "They always seem to know where the food is."

You take out your camera and zoom in on the lions. Their mouths are red with blood. You take a few shots and then Koinet moves off after the balloon again.

After following the balloon for another hour or so, the radio crackles and Pierre informs Koinet that they are about to land. Koinet speeds up so he is close by to help secure the balloon and so he can chase away any predators that might be in the area.

Koinet turns to you. "When the balloon is down, you can help us roll it up. Then once everything is back at camp I'll drive you to the lodge. How does that sound?"

"Perfect," you say.

Pierre and Marie make a soft landing. With the four of you working to pack up the balloon, rope, burners, and basket it only takes thirty minutes.

After dropping the trailer off at camp, Koinet and you drive off towards the lodge.

You wonder what your family is doing. Are they out somewhere looking for you? Have they got helicopters out scouring the Serengeti?

An hour later you get your answer. As you come out from behind a line of trees you meet your family coming in the opposite direction in the distinctive black and white zebra patterned Land Rovers the lodge uses. Your family are standing up in the back hanging on to the roll bars scanning the savannah for any sign of you.

Koinet stops his Land Rover in the track and you fling the door open. You can't believe your eyes. Your whole family is there. When they see you they yell for the Land Rover to stop and then rush towards you with outstretched arms calling your name. Tears of joy are flowing.

"So are we going to do another safari tomorrow?" you ask. "I know a couple of good spots we could check out."

Everyone laughs and gives you a big hug. Then they thank Koinet for driving you back.

Koinet smiles and then reaches into his pocket. He hands you a string of red beads. "Here, for you, a souvenir of your adventure."

"Thanks Koinet," you say, putting the beads around your neck. "I've got Pierre and Marie's address here in Tanzania. I'll send you some photos once I've got them printed. I've got a couple good ones of you."

Koinet smiles, waves one last time and drives off into the Serengeti.

You climb into the back of the black and white Land Rover. As the Land Rover starts to move off, you yell "STOP!"

The Land Rover skids to a halt. "What's the matter?" your family asks.

"I just wanted to make sure everyone is here. We wouldn't want to make the same mistake twice now would we?" You do a quick headcount. "Right, all present and accounted for. Let's get back to the lodge. I need a shower and a big bowl of ice cream."

Congratulations, you have completed this part of the journey and made it safely back to your family. But have you followed all the possible paths?

Now it is time to make another decision. Would you like to:

Go back to the very beginning of the story and try another route? **P1**

Or

Go to the list of choices and start reading from another part of the story? **P113**

You have decided to jump out of the balloon's basket onto the tree branch.

You are on your hands and knees on the inside wall of the basket. The tree branch is right there in front of you. The branch is reasonably wide and there is another smaller branch you'll be able to hang on to for stability.

You rise slowly into a crouch and then jump.

"No!" you hear Marie yell from behind you.

But it is too late to heed her warning. You are already out on the limb. You wrap your legs tight around the branch and grip the smaller branch for balance.

With the sudden reduction of weight, the basket shoots up and smacks you in the side.

Before you can regain your balance you are falling. You try to grab hold of another branch as you fall, but miss. Your head smacks into something hard. You head is spinning and your ribs ache.

The ground is coming up fast.

CRASH!

Everything goes dark.

You have made an unwise decision by climbing out of the balloon without first checking with the balloon's pilot. Remember when he said for you to stay below the rim of the basket? That was for a reason. The cane basket is designed to protect those inside it like a crash helmet protects your head if you fall when you are riding your bike.

Unfortunately this part of your story is over.

It is time to make another decision. Would you like to:

Go back to the very beginning of the story and try another path? **P1**

Or

Go back to your previous decision and make a different selection? **P92**

You have decided to stay in the basket.

You've made a wise decision by staying in the basket and waiting for instructions from the balloon's pilot. If you had leapt from the basket the sudden reduction in weight would have caused the balloon to shoot upward and would have put everyone at risk.

A gust of wind pulls at the balloon, tipping it further onto its side. Pierre leans out of the basket and kicks at a branch in an attempt to get the balloon clear of the snag.

With a sharp crack the branch gives way. The balloon swings forward, tipping the three of you into a heap in the bottom of the basket.

"We're clear," Pierre says struggling to regain his feet.

Marie and you untwist yourselves and stand up too. Pierre pulls a cord to release air from one of the side vents in the balloon. The more air he releases the further you drop.

"As soon as we hit the ground I will pull both flaps and release as much air as I can," Pierre says. "We may drag for a while so duck down and make sure you keep your head and arms below the rim. There are handholds inside the basket. Just hold on tight and wait until we stop."

You remember reading once that it isn't flying a balloon that is dangerous. It's the landings that are the tricky part. Now you understand why. But at least here in the Serengeti there aren't any power lines to get tangled in ... just trees and stampeding animals!

Bending your knees slightly, you get ready to duck down and brace yourself. The ground is getting closer.

"Almost there," Pierre says. "On my count, five ... four ... three ... two ... okay down everyone."

A jolt shudders through the basket as it hits the parched savannah. The basket tips on a slight angle and you can hear it scraping as the balloon drags it through the grass. Pierre has pulled both flaps fully open and air is rapidly spilling from the balloon.

After twenty seconds or so, the movement slows and then you finally stop altogether. The basket is resting on its side. When you look out, you see the balloon flapping in the light breeze as it lies on the ground shrinking rapidly as the air continues to escape.

Once enough air has escaped, Pierre tells you it is safe to climb out of the basket. You all run over to the top of the balloon and start rolling it up, forcing the remaining air out the mouth at the bottom.

It is less than a minute before Koinet drives up in the Land Rover. "How did you find your first flight?" he asks you as he joins in the rolling.

"The flight was wonderful," you say. "I'm not so sure about the landing."

Koinet smiles, "I thought I might have to rescue you all for a moment."

"Ignition wouldn't fire for some reason," Pierre says. "We might have to go into town for parts before we launch again."

The four of you set to work packing everything up and loading it into the covered trailer attached to the back of the Land Rover. Once everything has been put away, you jump into the back seat with Marie.

On the drive back you look through the shots you got on your camera.

Marie leans over and has a look too. "Some of those are great," she says. "You could be a wildlife photographer when you get older if you keep taking pictures like these."

You are pleased that a professional thinks your pictures are good. Maybe you will study to be a photographer one day. What a great job that would be, travelling to exotic countries and taking photos of the many beautiful and unusual animals there are in the world.

After getting back to camp, Pierre takes the faulty burner apart and finds the part that needs replacing. It's just a simple valve. He gives the damaged piece to Koinet who will pick up a replacement in town after he drops you back at the lodge.

You are pleased to be heading back to the lodge at last. You miss your family and are sure they will be worrying themselves sick.

Koinet unhooks the trailer and climbs in behind the wheel. You sit with you camera at the ready in the passenger seat. Hopefully there will be some photo opportunities on the way to the lodge.

Two hours and thirty eight photographs later, the Land Rover pulls into the lodge compound. You see your family members talking to a man in uniform. When they see you, they all rush over and surround you. They are asking you so many questions at once you can't hear yourself think.

"Slow down," you say. "I'll answer all your questions in a few minutes. Let's find a computer so I can transfer my photographs. Then I'll give you a slide show and tell you all about my adventure in lion country."

Congratulations, this part of your story has come to an end with you safe return to the lodge despite the many dangers you faced. Have you followed all the possible paths yet?

It is time to make a decision. Would you like to:

Go back to the very beginning of the story and take another path? **P1**

Or

Go to the list of choices and choose another part of the book start reading from? **P113**

You have decided to sneak down to the lodge and try to help your family.

You can't bring yourself to run off and leave your family. There must be something you can do. You zoom in again with your camera to see what is going on. You even take a few shots of the poachers so you have some evidence for the police.

It looks like the poacher gang is forcing the lodge guests to turn out their pockets and take off any jewelry they are wearing. You look on as your family and the other guests put their valuables into a bag being held out by one of the poachers.

All the gang members have their backs to you, so you sprint down the hill and stop outside the fence just by the gate. There are only narrow spaces between the poles, but they are big enough for you to look through into the compound. You lie on your belly and listen.

The gang leader is yelling at the lodge guests.

"You better give us everything!" he shouts. "If we find out you are lying, we will beat you!"

One of the male guests reaches down into his sock and pulls out a wallet. He tosses it over to the poacher.

"Is there any more?" the poacher asks as he points his gun at each guest in turn.

The guests are shaking their heads. Some are crying.

"We've given you everything," an older woman says.

"Please don't hurt us."

What will the poachers do? Will they harm the guests? What can you do to help?

Then you remember that there is a satellite phone in the lodge's office. You heard one of the staff telling a guest that it works just like a normal cell phone, but didn't rely on cell phone towers. Instead it bounced its signal off satellites.

If you could get into the office without the poachers seeing you, you could phone for help. But how?

You study the compound from outside the fence. The office is the last room on the right hand side of the main building. The poachers and the guests are on the veranda near the dining room on the left.

Then you have an idea.

Staying low, you run through the gate and hide behind the first of the lodge's Land Rovers. You check to see if the poachers still have their backs turned and then sprint over to the poacher's truck. It is higher off the ground than the Land Rovers so you hide behind the truck's tires, otherwise if a poacher turns around, he will be able to see your legs under the vehicle.

Your luck is holding.

You take a peek under the truck. The men are now searching the guests to make sure they haven't kept anything back. You sprint to the next Land Rover.

"What about this?" a poacher screams at a woman. "Why didn't you give us this ring?"

"I can't get it off," the woman cries.

Another poacher comes over to investigate. He grabs the woman's hand and starts to pull.

"Ouch that hurts!" the woman yells.

While the men try to get the woman's ring off her finger, their attention is distracted. You run over and hide behind the last Land Rover in the row.

The office door is just up the steps on your right. Luckily the door is ajar.

As you peek around the back of the vehicle, one of the male guests spots you. He turns his head to disguise the fact that he has seen you, but then turns back and gives you the slightest of nods as if to say he knows what you are trying to do.

You just need the poachers to keep looking the other way long enough for you to cross the last part of the compound, climb the four steps onto the veranda, and duck through the office door.

The male guest sees your problem. The distance you have to cover might be too far to run without the poachers seeing you. Some sort of distraction is required. He winks at you and nods again.

The next thing you know the man is on the ground rolling around in agony clutching his chest. All the poachers stop what they are doing and look at the man. A woman drops to her knees and tries to help. She looks horrified.

Not wasting any time, you sprint across the compound,

run up the steps and rush through the office door. A quick peek out the window and you see the man sitting up on the ground, his wife is mopping his sweaty brow with a tissue.

Now where is that phone?

Then you see it sitting on top of the filing cabinet behind the main counter. Next to the filing cabinet on a cork notice board is a list of emergency numbers. Police is second on the list. You punch in the numbers. Thankfully, the woman who answers speaks a little English. She understands the words emergency, poachers, guns, Habari Lodge, and help.

"Will send police," she says.

You breathe a sigh of relief. Help is on the way. As long as the poachers don't hurt your family before the police arrive, everything should be okay.

But how long will it take for the police to get here? The lodge must be at least an hour from town, if not more. Will the poachers still be here in an hour?

You peek out the window again. It looks like the gang is getting ready to leave. Apart from the bag of goodies they have collected from the various guests, a couple of the gang members have just come out of the kitchen carrying boxes of groceries.

The leader is yelling at them to hurry. While two of the gang guards the guests, the others go back inside the lodge to get more stuff.

You want the poachers to leave, but you also want the police to be able to catch them. What can you do to make that happen? After thinking for a moment, you decide to take a chance.

You check what is happening outside. When all the poachers are looking the other way, you sprint back over to their truck. The truck's fuel tank is on the side facing away from the poachers. You unscrew its cap and grab a couple of handfuls of dirt and pour them into the tank. Then you screw the cap on again.

Hopefully the poachers will get their truck out of the compound, but the dirt will block their fuel line before they get too far away so the police can find them.

You run back towards the office.

"Stop!" a poacher yells.

You've been seen. You run into the office, slam the door, and push the lock button in the middle of the door knob. You slide your camera along the floor and under the sofa to keep the poachers from stealing it.

The poacher who saw you doesn't even bother to try the door handle. Instead, he kicks the door with such force that it flies back and hits the wall so hard that the window in the door breaks, showering the floor with shards of glass.

You look around, but there is nowhere to hide. "Come here!" the poacher yells as he grabs your arm and drags you out onto the veranda.

There is no point in resisting. If you do, you will only get hurt.

You try to regain your feet as the man pulls you towards

the other guests. Then he flings you down on the ground at your family's feet.

"Stay!" the poacher says. "Stay here or I will shoot you!"

You look at your family and shrug. Their eyes are huge. No doubt they are wondering where you came from.

"I'm back," you say. "I was ..."

"Shut up! No talking!" the poacher yells.

You can see the anger on the poacher's face so you do as he says and keep your mouth shut. There is no point in getting shot when you are less than an hour from being rescued by the police. You move over and sit with your back to the wall.

The gang is loading everything they can onto the back of the truck, food, alcohol, TV's, even a table and chairs from the dining room. You can hear the sound of things breaking as the gang ransacks the place.

Once the men have loaded all they can on the truck, the leader yells for his men to climb aboard. Then he turns to the guests. "If you follow, you will die!"

By the crazy look on his face, you don't doubt he is telling the truth. Your body is shaking with fear. All you want is for these horrible men to leave. You look at your feet and keep quiet.

Once all the men are on the truck, you cross your fingers that their truck will start. With all the dirt you put into the fuel tank, you can't imagine them getting very far.

When the truck starts first try, you relax a little. Then with a puff of black smoke and a couple of shots into the air, the poachers drive out of the compound and head off across the savannah.

"Where did you come from?" your family members ask.

You are about to tell them how you came to be in the compound when you hear the poacher's truck splutter and then backfire.

"Oh no ... not yet ... please truck, don't stop now," you say. "This is too close to the lodge. They may come back."

As your family asks you what you mean, you see a couple of the men get down off the back deck and walk around to the front of the truck. They start looking into the engine compartment.

"I put dirt in the truck's fuel tank," you explain.

"Quick, lets close the gate," the lodge manager says. "Unfortunately they've taken all our weapons."

As a couple of the men move across the compound, you hear a steady whump, whump, whumping sound.

"What is that?" a woman guest asks.

The sound is getting closer.

"Sounds like a helicopter," the lodge manager says. He turns and looks at you. "Did you call the police?"

You nod. "I used the phone in the office."

The police helicopter hovers over the compound and then slowly descends into its center. The guests run back onto the veranda as the dust swirls around.

The lodge manager runs over and has a quick word with

one of the policemen, then runs back to join the others. The helicopter lifts off again and heads toward the poacher's truck.

"Well those poachers will be out of action for a while thanks to your bravery," the lodge manger says as he rests his hand on your shoulder. "Even those idiots won't be stupid enough to argue with the big machine gun the police have on board that chopper."

Your family gathers around. They all give you a big hug.

"Can I use your computer?" you ask the lodge manager. "I've got some evidence the police can use on my camera."

"Sure," he says.

You run up the steps and into the office. Once you've retrieved your camera from under the couch, you take out the memory card and slot it into the lodge's laptop. You take a copy of the pictures and paste them onto the desktop.

"There you go. Now the police will have all the evidence they need to convict those awful men."

"Well you've certainly done very well for someone lost in lion country," the manager says.

All your family are smiling. They seem to agree. "We'll have to leave you behind more often!"

Congratulations you have saved the day. You have not only successfully made it back to the lodge and your family, but you've helped capture a nasty gang of poachers. Well done!

This part of your adventure is over. Have you followed all the possible paths yet? Have you travelled with the baboons? Flown in a balloon? Met the film-makers? Seen all the animals?

It is now time to make another decision. Would you like to:

Go back to the very beginning of the story and try another path? **P1**

Or

Go to the list of choices and choose another place to start reading from **P113**

You have decided to go back to the Maasai village for help.

You are shocked at what is happening in the lodge, but you realize that on your own you are unlikely to be of much help. The poachers are armed with semi-automatic weapons and knives. What is the point of you getting caught? What help would you be then?

You start jogging back the way you came. If you can keep up the pace, you might get back to the village in an hour and a half, assuming you don't run into trouble along the way.

You take a good drink of water and then jog for ten minutes, then you walk until you've cooled down. You drink again and then jog again.

After repeating this jog, walk, drink routine three or four times you stop to rest and look around the savannah for potential danger. The second time you stop for a rest, you see something a little worrying. It is only for a moment, but you are sure you saw a tail swish above the swaying grass a few hundred paces to your right.

Was that a lion's tail you just saw? Is it stalking you?

Where is the nearest tree? You see one you think you can climb fifty paces off the track to your left. Should you run or walk? If you run will a lion sprint out after you? You have no doubt you'd lose if it came to a straight footrace.

You start moving towards the tree at a walk, trying not to show the panic that is thumping in your chest. When you are about half way to the tree, you turn and look back. There is no sign of a tail, but the long grass just over a hundred paces away is moving.

You want to run but your knees feel weak. You look at the tree and plan exactly where you are going to place your hands and feet when you make your break. You carefully loop the strap of your spear over your shoulder to free up your hands for climbing.

When you are twenty paces from the tree you take off, pumping your legs and arms for all they are worth. You don't look back. That would only slow you down.

You hit the tree trunk with your right foot and use it to spring up and grab a lower limb. With the upward momentum of your leap, you pull with your arms and hook your knee over the limb and swing up so you are sitting. Grabbing onto the main trunk you pull yourself up into a standing position and reach for the next branch.

You hear something running thought the dry grass. It is getting nearer.

You don't look anywhere but up to the next branch, up to your next step. Your grip slips and a big splinter jabs into your palm. Blood trickles down your arm, but you don't have time to worry about that now. You scramble higher and higher into the tree.

Now it's time to fight for your life. You turn and wedge yourself in the crook of two branches and pull the spear off your shoulder. You spin the point downward as the lion starts up the trunk. It is a large male with a magnificent mane of golden hair. Around its mouth and chin the hairs are almost white. The lion digs his claws into the trunk. Powerful muscles in the cat's front legs pull the body up past the first branch. The cat's eyes are yellow with narrow black pupils.

It stares at you and snarls. You can smell the cat's bad breath and see its huge front teeth.

"No!" you yell at the top of your voice. "Go away!"

The only thing stopping the lion from lunging at you are a couple of stout branches blocking the way. You yell again and jab your spear downwards.

Then you hear gunshots. The cat hears them too. Both of you look for the source of the noise. Another shot pings off the ground near the base of the tree. A dark green Land Rover is tooting it horn as it nears.

The cat looks up at you, roars one last time, and then slides back down the tree and sprints off into the long grass.

Your hands shake. Sweat drips off your forehead. You sit between two branches for a moment, afraid that if you don't you might fall.

"You okay up there?" a deep male voice yells.

A man dressed in uniform is at the base of the tree looking up at you. He wears a green cap with a yellow badge sewn onto its front. Over his shoulder is a rifle. His dark skin shines like ebony and his smile is the brightest and friendliest you've ever seen.

You smile back at him. "I am now that you are here!" You loop your spear's strap over your shoulder and start down. When you reach the ground your knees nearly buckle.

"Here let me help you," the man says taking hold of your elbow. "Come and sit, you are probably in shock."

You allow the man to lead you over to his vehicle. When he sees the blood on your hand he pulls out a first aid kit, removes the splinter and patches you up.

Four other men are standing around the Land Rover. All are dressed in the same uniform and carrying automatic weapons. On the side of the Land Rover is the same yellow and green logo as on the man's cap.

"Are you wildlife rangers?" you ask.

"Yes," the man replies. "We are looking for poachers. What are you doing out here alone?"

Then you remember your family. You'd been so busy trying to stay alive that for a moment there you'd forgotten all about them.

"The poachers are at Habari Lodge robbing the guests," you say.

"Habari Lodge?"

You explain what you saw and how you were on your way to the Maasai village for help when you saw the lion and made a dash for the tree.

After listening to your story, the ranger has a word to his men and they all pile into the Land Rover. You are directed to sit in the back seat between two men. The last man jumps onto the back where a machine gun is mounted on a tripod. Its barrel points over the roof.

"You've got a lot of fire power here," you say to one of the rangers.

"Believe me, when it comes to dealing with these heavily armed criminals we need it."

The driver turns the Land Rover around and starts down the track towards Habari Lodge. On the drive you fill the head ranger in on everything you saw, the number of guests and staff at the lodge, and everything else you can remember about the poachers and the lodge's layout.

The ranger's Land Rover stops behind a row of bushes on a rise overlooking the lodge. It is close to the spot where you first noticed the poachers. Their flatbed truck is still in the compound.

The head ranger studies the situation with his binoculars. The poachers have tied up the guests on the veranda and are loading stuff onto their truck.

"I think they are getting ready to leave," he tells you.

The chief ranger wanders over to chat with his men. Then he comes back to you. "We are going to wait until they come out of the compound before we strike. This should reduce the chance of injury to the guests and staff."

You nod. It sounds like the right thing to do. The last thing you want is for your family to get hurt.

"We will leave you up here during the attack. After it is safe we will come back and pick you up."

One of the men rushes over to the head ranger and has a few words.

"It is time," the head ranger tells you. "Stay here. Hopefully we won't be long."

You are about to be left in the Serengeti once again. Only this time you will have a ring side seat to something few people will see on holiday, a poacher group being brought to justice.

The faint sound of a motor starting brings all the rangers to the alert. All but two of the rangers jump into the vehicle. The other two get on the back deck to operate the big machine gun.

Inside the vehicle, the men roll down their window and point their guns outside ready for action.

"Let's go!" one of the men on top of the ranger's Land Rover yells.

The ranger's vehicle revs up and races down the hill. You pull your camera out of you bag and move to a spot where you can watch the action below.

The poachers have come out of the lodge and have turned onto a track that heads west towards the hills. The rangers are gaining on them. You snap pictures of the action.

When the ranger's big gun opens up, the ground around the flatbed truck erupts with puffs of dirt. Some of the bullets hit their front tires. Their truck swerves sharply, and then starts to roll. The men on the back leap for their lives just as the truck lands on its side and slides through the dirt.

Rangers pile out of their Land Rover and surround the poachers. Two are pulled from the wrecked cab. With a machine gun pointing at them, the poachers see sense and give up. They raise their hands above their heads and sink to their knees.

It is not long before the rangers have the poachers in handcuffs.

You figure it is safe to go down to the lodge, so you put your camera into your daypack and pick up your spear. You can't wait to see your family.

When you enter the compound all the guests and staff are lined up along the veranda, their hands tied in front of them. Your family are shocked to see you. They have heard all the shooting but don't know what is going on.

You start untying people. As people are untied, they help others. Everyone gives you a big hug as you release them and ask how it is that you are here.

"I'll explain later," you say. "Once I've loaded my pictures onto my laptop, I'll give you a slide show and tell you the whole story."

You wave your family towards the dining room. "Let's all go and have something nice and cold to drink. It sounds like everyone's got a tale to tell. This has turned out to be quite some holiday!"

Congratulations, you have made it safely back to your

family. This part of your story is over, but have you followed all the possible paths and had all the possible adventures?

It is time to make another decision. Would you like to:

Go back to the very beginning of the story and try another path? **P1**

Or

Go to the list of choices and start reading from another place? **P113**

List of Choices

Special Preview - Pirate Island

Your family is on holiday at a lush tropical island resort in the Caribbean. But you're not in the mood to sit around the pool with the others, you want to go exploring. You have heard that pirate treasure has been found in these parts and you are keen to find some too. You put a few supplies into your daypack, fill your drinking bottle with water, grab your mask and snorkel, and head towards the beach.

You like swimming, but you've been planning this treasure hunt for months and now is as good a time as any to start. The beach outside the resort stretches off in both directions.

To your right it runs past the local village, where children laugh as they splash and play in the water. Palm trees line the shore and brightly colored fishing boats rest on the sand above the high tide mark. Past the village, way off in the distance, is a lighthouse.

To your left, the sandy beach narrows quickly and soon becomes a series of rocky outcrops jutting into the sea. Steep cliffs rise up from the rocky shore to meet the stone walls of an old and crumbling fortress.

You have four hours before your family expect you back.

After deciding to turn right and walk out to the lighthouse you make your way down to the hard, wet sand where the walking will be easier.

Off in the distance, past the local village, the palm trees

gradually thin out and the lush vegetation gives way to low sand dunes, scrub, and hardy grasses. A narrow sand spit, with a lighthouse on its far end, juts out into the ocean. The spit curves around in a gentle arc, forming a protected bay sheltered from the full force of the ocean beyond. Seabirds dive into the bay's sparkling blue waters as they hunt for fish.

As you walk down the beach, you pass resort guests lying on beach towels, swimming in the ocean, and playing games in the sand. You're not interested in all that, you want to find treasure.

You're pretty sure there is unlikely to be any treasure so close to civilization, so you pick up the pace. You want to get as far away from the others as you can and check out the windswept sand spit where it's far more likely you'll find treasure. What clever pirate would bury his treasure so close to the village?

Coconut palms line the shoreline and you hear birds and other animals in the jungle beyond the trees. Out in the bay, small fish are leaping out of the water trying to escape bigger fish below. Hungry gulls dive bomb the little fish from above. Then even bigger fish are leaping from the water, and you wonder what is chasing them. You've never seen so many fish and birds in one place before.

After walking for about half an hour you reach the sand spit. The jungle further inland starts to thin out and you can see water through the trees on the other side of the peninsula. Gradually even the palm trees are left behind and the only plants you see are low scrub and tough grasses whose roots cling for dear life onto the sand.

An old weather-beaten sign explains that the sand spit is the nesting place for migratory birds. It asks you to watch where you walk so you don't disturb any nests by mistake.

Not wanting to frighten or harm the nesting birds, you are careful where you step, keeping to the water's edge and away from the dunes. Small grey birds with pale yellow plumage on their chests scurry around, screeching at you whenever you get too close. You admire these mother birds for their bravery in chasing off something so much larger than themselves.

The sand spit is littered with bleached shells that have been washed up over time. In the wet sand you can see bubbles. The bubbles and the old shells lying about make you think there must be quite a few shellfish hiding under the sand. You dig in your toes and sure enough a small scallop is uncovered. You pick up the shell and inspect it. It is a half circle with ridges in the shell radiating out like a child's drawing of the sun. The other side of the shell is the same and you notice a small hinge that holds the two side of the cream and pink shell together.

After looking at the shell for a few moments, you drop it back onto the wet sand and are amazed at how it manages to wriggle its way back under the sand and disappear. Then, with one last bubble, it's gone.

The sun is hot so you pull your floppy hat and sunglasses out of your daypack and put them on. You are pleased you brought water and take a long sip. The sunglasses make it much easier for you to look though the water to the seabed below. You decide to walk with your feet in the shallows to cool off a bit as you continue towards the lighthouse.

A flash of color glints from under the crystal clear water a little way off shore. You stop and stare, trying to see what has caused the sparkle. Little fish dart left and right.

Was it just the light catching the side of a silver fish, or could this be the treasure you are looking for?

You drop your gear and wade in to the water to get a better look at whatever is reflecting the light. By the time you are waist deep you realize the water is far deeper than you first thought.

Back on the beach you take your snorkeling gear out of your bag and strip down to your bathing suit and then wade out into the bay. After rinsing out your mask, you fit it to your face, pop in the snorkel's mouthpiece and stick your head under the water to try to see what is glimmering.

Out in deeper water you see a twinkle of sunlight reflecting off something. The glimmer isn't moving so you figure it isn't a fish. You lie on your stomach and paddle out along the surface with your face in the water, breathing through your mouthpiece, until you are directly over what looks like a gold coin resting on the sandy bottom.

You can feel your heart beating in your chest. You can't

believe your eyes. Could this be your first discovery?

After taking a deep breath you dive. Down and down you go. The water is so clear everything looks much closer than it actually is. As you dive you kick with all your strength, scooping water with your cupped hands. You are so deep the pressure is starting to hurt your ears.

Just as your hand reaches for the coin, a shadow races along the sandy bottom. The shadow is huge and moving quickly. You snatch the coin off the sand and flip onto your back, looking for whatever it is that is causing the shadow. You hope it isn't a shark.

It only takes a moment to find what you are looking for. Near the surface, a manta ray flies like a bird, its wings barely moving as it glides through the water. The ray's mouth is as wide as the front grill of a car and it wings stretch out and then curve up at their tips. Behind the ray swishes a snake-like tail.

You relax a little. You know that despite being big, manta rays aren't dangerous. You watch entranced as the manta ray passes, but then your lungs start to burn. You push off the bottom and head for the surface, desperate for air, clutching the coin in your hand.

After your head breaks the surface, you spit out your mouthpiece and gulp in air. After a few deep breaths you take off your mask and hook its strap over your wrist and start dog paddling back towards the beach, happy with your discovery.

Sitting in the sand at the edge of the water, you study the coin. It is quite rough and looks handmade, not perfectly round like modern coins. On one side there is an old style cross. You're pleased you did an online search for treasure before coming on holiday and remember that this type of cross is called a Crusader's Cross, which signified the union of the Catholic Church and the government of Spain back in the old days.

What's even more exciting is the picture of a Lion and a Castle on the back of the coin. This means you've found a gold Spanish doubloon! The doubloon was a common coin at the time of the Spanish conquistadors. The Spanish exchanged them for trade goods in the New World for nearly two hundred years.

Have you found part of a pirate's treasure? Or is it a coin washed up from some ancient shipwreck? The coin looks pretty knocked around.

You're excited to go and look for more coins, but just as you put on your snorkel again, you see a triangular grey fin cruising back and forth along the beach. It's hard to tell if the fin is a shark or a dolphin. You wait for a while to see if you can get a better look at what sort of fish the fin belongs to, but whatever it is swims off before you can identify it.

You wait a few more minutes to see if it comes back, but it doesn't. You decide it's not safe to go back into the water and are pleased that you decided to keep walking rather than go back into the water. The fin has returned and is cruising just off the beach. It was not a dolphin but a big and hungry looking shark. Smaller fish in the shark's path are jumping out of the water in their attempt to get away. This has brought the birds back.

You tuck the gold doubloon safely away in your pocket and start walking towards the lighthouse, eager to find more treasure.

As the spit curves around, you can see the resort and the local village far across the bay. The houses of the village are small compared to the multi-story buildings of the new resort. You can just make out the small fishing boats pulled up onto the sand. Wet fishing nets glisten in the sun as they dry, strung out on poles in the warmth of the sun.

You are so busy looking back at the village as you walk you almost step on a nest. It's only the desperate call of the mother bird that alerts you to it.

Then you hear a voice call out. "Hey watch it!"

When you turn towards the voice you see a boy about the same age as you carrying a net bag of shellfish. Around the boy's neck is a string of shells. His skin is burnt brown by the sun.

"Sorry," you tell the boy and walk around the nest. "I was busy looking at the village and not watching where I was going."

The boy shrugs. "These birds are endangered you know. Didn't you read the sign?"

You explain how you've come out here on the spit to

look for pirate treasure, not to harm the birds. You ask the boy if he has ever found any gold coins out here on the sand spit when he's been digging for shellfish.

"No," the boy says shaking his head. "But the village elders tell stories about pirates and treasure, stories that their parents told them. I've heard them repeated all my life."

"Could you tell me what you've heard?" you ask the boy.

"I could, but I've got to get these scallops back to the village. My mother will be annoyed if I'm late."

You nod your head and frown.

"But if you want to come by the village when you get back from your walk, I can tell you some stories. How does that sound?"

"That would be great," you tell the boy.

"My house is the one nearest the red and blue fishing boat. You shouldn't have any problem finding it."

You thank the boy and he heads off toward the village, turning once to give you a wave. You carry on toward the lighthouse.

As the sun rises higher in the sky, the heat of the day increases. You take the water bottle out of your pack and drink. The water is lukewarm but at least it's wet. As you drink, you watch a family of crabs scuttle sideways across the sand. Their eyes are black and stand out bead-like on stems. Their bodies are bright orange and shiny. When you approach for a closer look the crabs turn towards you and lift their pincers into the air for protection. You imagine the nip those big pincers could give you and stay well clear. One crab advances on you, and you laugh at his antics as he waves his arms around and snaps his claws.

You walk around the crabs and pick up the pace. Before long you reach the lighthouse.

The lighthouse sits on a base of large rocks concreted together to form a wide flat platform. The platform is taller than you, but a narrow set of steps lead up to the base of the building on one side. Rusted handrails allow you a handhold on the slippery algae covered steps.

The lighthouse tower is white with bright red stripes running around it. A structure made of glass windows with a peaked roof and a white balcony crown its top. There is a brass plaque mounted on the outside wall near a big steel door.

You climb up the steps to investigate further.

The brass plaque has gone a little green over time, but the engraved words are still quite clear. You step a little closer and read.

Beware of the sea. For under these calm waters lay many shattered dreams.

As you think about the words written on the plaque you walk over to the lighthouse's door. Its surface is bubbled with rust, but it hinges are big and strong and its paint is fresh and white. You turn the handle to see if the door is unlocked, but it does not move.

From the base of the lighthouse you get a great view of

the surrounding area. As you look back in the direction from which you've come, you see that the tide is on its way in and the water is coming further and further up the beach with every minute that passes. You also see a narrow path, paved with crushed shells on the other side of the sand spit. It looks like it leads back toward the village through the jungle. You're not sure where the shell covered path goes, so you decide to head back the way you came.

You climb down from the lighthouse platform and walk down to the beach. The tide forces you to walk higher up the sand to avoid getting wet. You wonder how much higher the water will come up before you get back to the resort. Already piles of seaweed and small pieces of driftwood lay near the high tide mark.

You figure this is as high as the water will come up so you relax and get into your stride. You probably only have an hour or so before you will be expected back at the resort. You don't want to get into trouble because then you might not get to go out on your own to explore any more of the island.

As you walk along the high tide mark you watch the antics of the birds. Most of the time you're alerted by the parent birds whenever you get close to a nest.

When you look down the beach, the resort seems a long way away. You didn't realize how far you'd walked so you speed up a little in the hope of making up some time.

You hear a splash out in the water and turn to see what is

going on. Now there are not one, but four sinister grey fins swimming back and forth along the beach. Only little fish are jumping out of the water at first, but then even bigger fish are leaping for their lives. When the seabirds dive in to feast on the sardines stirred up by the sharks, the ocean is turned into a battle ground for survival. Everything that moves is searching for a meal.

Walking so far has made you a little bit weary. You want to stop and take a break, but you also know your family will worry if you are late.

Not much further down the beach, you hear a frantic chirping. In front of you a mother bird is telling you off for getting too close to her nest. As you move inland a little to give the nest a wide berth you notice a small mound of stones. The stack looks like a marker of some sort. It certainly isn't a natural formation.

You walk towards the pile, curious to see what it is.

The mound is nearly waist high. The stone on top is flat and has a compass rose engraved onto its surface. A needle on the rose points towards the jungle. You stand behind the cairn and look in the direction of the arrow. It points to a tall tree a couple of hundred paces into the jungle. The cairn has lichen growing on the shady sides, indicating to you that it has been there for quite some time. You scrabble around in the sand at the base of the cairn in case something is buried nearby but you find nothing. You're not quite sure what the arrow indicates, but you hope it could be a clue to finding some treasure. Is the arrow pointing to the big tree, or something else?

You look up at the big tree and then back at the lighthouse behind you to get your bearings. You know that once you enter the jungle you won't be able to see the tree or the lighthouse from the ground. You need to work out a way to keep walking straight and not end up going around in circles.

You find a smaller tree on the edge of the jungle that is in line with both the lighthouse and the big tree in the jungle and head for that. It is only a few hundred steps across scrub and low, grass covered dunes to the small tree. Once you get to the small tree, you look back across the dunes at the lighthouse and then pick another tree further into the jungle that is in line with the lighthouse and the smaller tree you first used as a landmark. By repeating this procedure you figure you can keep your direction straight enough to find the big tree.

The jungle is cool and shady. When you look up, only small patches of sky can be seen between the outstretched branches of the many trees and shrubs.

A small red headed, yellow breasted hummingbird hovers near a bright pink flower, sucking nectar with its long beak. The broad leafed plant reminds you of the lilies back home only much, much larger.

You stop and listen, amazed by all the unusual sounds. High in the canopy, you hear a loud squawking. It takes a moment for your eyes to adjust to the low light, but before long you see a toucan with its black and white body, yellow beak and bright blue eyes singing for a mate. Two bright green parrots sit on a branch nearby, plucking at red berries with their strong pink and grey beaks. The parrot's cheeks have a patch of red making it look as though they are blushing.

You would like to stay and watch, but you know that you need to get moving. You also need to focus, otherwise you might become disorientated and lose your way.

After repeating your technique for keeping your course straight a few times you finally come to the big tree. Its root system is like a swarm of giant snakes, twisting and turning as they wind around and then finally go underground. From this unusual root system a large trunk emerges covered in moss and lichen and small delicate ferns.

You raise your head and look up. The tree trunk seems to go on forever. Vines hang from above and colonies of other plants live in the tree's branches. You've never seen so many things growing on a single tree. Then you notice that some of the vines hanging from the tree have been woven into a ladder of sorts. Is this what the arrow on the rock was pointing you towards? Or are you imagining things? Maybe this is just how these particular vines grow?

Through some shrubs to your left you see a pathway covered in white shells that lead off into the jungle in the direction of the village.

The vines hanging down from the tree are about as thick as your thumb and seem strong enough to hold your weight when you pull down on them. Many of the vines have twisted around each other in such a way that there are plenty of footholds within reach. You have always been pretty good at climbing trees but you have never had a go at climbing one so large before.

The higher you climb, the more vines you have to hold on to. It is a long way up to the first branch. A couple of times during the climb, you stop to rest your aching legs.

When you finally reach the first branch you sit and look down. Everything below looks a long way away. Parrots squawk and zip past you on their way to the next bunch of berries. There is a bed of ferns in the crook of the tree that provides you with something soft to lean against.

You lay back and rest against the fern fronds. As you do so, you stare up into the higher branches. You are amazed at how much wildlife there is in the tree. You've counted six different birds so far, numerous butterflies, moths, flying insects of all sorts and even a small rodent of some sort.

You can see for miles from your vantage point. Then you notice something odd. There is a short piece of brass pipe lashed to one of the bigger branches with old hemp rope. The rope has been varnished to protect it from the elements. You are curious as to why anyone would put something like that up in the tree.

Holding onto a branch for support, you stand up and

look more closely at the pipe. Then closing one eye, like you would when looking through a telescope, you peer through one end to see if it is pointing at something in particular.

The only thing you can see through the pipe is the top of the little island that sits offshore from the old fortress.

Is this a clue left by the pirates? Is the island the place you should be exploring if you want to find treasure?

You are lying in the crook of the tree again, thinking about this new development, when you notice one of the branches above you is moving. It is wriggling. Then you realize it isn't a branch at all, but a large python! The mottled pattern on the snake's back helps it blend in with the foliage so well, you nearly missed it altogether. The bad news is that the snake is heading down the tree towards you far quicker than you like.

The snake is big, maybe not big enough to swallow you whole, but it is certainly big enough to create a serious problem if it wrapped its strong muscular body around you. It could strangle you, or even make you fall out of the tree. You've read that python bites, although not poisonous, can cause serious infection because of the bacteria in their mouths.

You grab onto the vines again, ready to scoot back down, but then the snake turns off onto a higher branch and twists and turns its way out to the end where a nest made of twigs and moss has been built by a bird.

You admire how easily the snake makes it way out to the

end of the branch. Then the snake's head disappears over the lip of the bird's nest only to return with an egg in its mouth. The snakes mouth hinges back to allow the egg to slide into its throat before it goes back for another. The lump in the snake's belly is easily visible. A mother bird sits on a branch nearby squawking in distress, helpless to save her babies.

There is a piece of broken branch lodged in the crook of the tree, and you feel sorry for the mother bird. You grab the branch and hurl it up towards the snake as hard as you can. The lump of wood barely clips the snake's tail before falling to the ground, but it is enough to give the snake a fright.

The problem is, now the snake is headed your way, and it's moving fast!

If you sit still, will the snake slither right on by you? Or, in its frightened state, will it give you a nasty bite and potentially ruin your holiday.

The snake moves quickly down the tree. You press your back into the bed of ferns and freeze, hoping it won't notice you.

The snake twists and turns along the branch until it is directly overhead. You want to turn your face up so you can see what it is doing, but you don't want to move and give yourself away.

The snake's scales feel incredibly smooth and cool as they slide over your shoulder and brush your neck. Is the snake about to coil itself around your windpipe and strangle you? Then you see its head moving further down and you feel the weight of the snake's body pressing on your legs.

The tail gives your neck a final flick as it passes and the snake disappears from view further down the tree. A drop of sweat runs down your cheek.

That was a little too close for comfort. Still, it was worth climbing the tree for the clue you've gained about needing to go to the island. Or is this just some game the locals play on the tourists to keep them coming back?

In either case you are eager to find out. You grab the vines and start your descent, but find that locating the footholds are much harder when climbing down. You wrap a vine around one ankle and search desperately with your other foot until you locate a place to stand. After resting your arms, you lower yourself down again and repeat the process.

Your hands and arms are tired from holding your weight and your hands are getting slippery with sweat. When you start to slip you manage to hook your arm through a loop to stop yourself from falling. Climbing down isn't as easy as you thought it would be.

Still you have no choice but to continue. You dry one hand at a time on your shirt then start your descent once more. But before long you are sliding down faster than you want. Your hands are burning from the friction. Luckily you are almost down when you let go and fall into the soft undergrowth. You roll as your feet hit the ground but still the wind is knocked out of you.

You lie on the ground and catch your breath. Two close calls in a row have given you the shakes.

After resting a minute you decide to head back towards the resort. You want to see if you can get out to the island and see if there really is treasure hidden there somewhere.

You also wonder if the boy from the village might have some useful information.

You go to the shell covered path and start walking. After walking for half an hour you come to a small stream and refill your water bottle. At little further on, you hear the sound of chickens clucking and village children playing.

You want to find the village boy you met on the beach and see if you can get more information. The stories that the village elders tell the children about the pirates that sailed these seas many years ago interest you. It might contain a clue about where to find more doubloons.

As you enter the village, you are surrounded by curious children, dogs, and even the odd chicken. The older children want to give you high fives, and run off laughing after slapping your upraised hand. Then the younger children do the same, imitating their older brothers and sisters.

You notice many of the dogs look similar. They are mainly tan in colour, have short legs and long bodies. Some follow the children on the lookout for scraps they might drop, and some lie in the shade with their tongues hanging out.

As you head towards the beach, you keep an eye out for the red and blue boat the boy described. Then you see it pulled up on the beach.

In a hut nearest the boat, a woman who you assume is the boy's mother is outside stirring a large pot set on a metal stand over a small fire. A man wearing shorts and sunglasses, probably the boy's father, sits in a chair a few yards away.

You approach the woman and ask her if her son is around. She tells you that he has gone off to collect coconuts. She points towards a group of trees up the beach and you see a small figure up a coconut palm swinging a machete.

"Thank you," you say to the woman and trot off to speak to the boy.

When you reach the tree the boy has climbed, you watch out for falling coconuts. Five are already on the ground near your feet.

"Hello," you yell up to the boy.

He looks down and smiles. Then he chops down two more coconuts before walking down the tree trunk using only his hands and feet.

When the boy reaches the ground he picks up one of the coconuts and with skilful use of the machete chops off the fibrous outer husk until he gets to the hard shell of the nut itself.

With a quick chop he opens a small hole on one end of the coconut and hands it to you.

"Here, drink," he says.

You take the coconut and bring the hole to your lips and let the sweet milk flow into your mouth. It is the most refreshing thing you have ever tasted.

When you have finished drinking the milk, the boy takes the coconut and cracks it open with the blunt side of his machete. Then he levers a piece of white flesh off the brown shell and hands it to you.

You bite right in and chew the piece up. The boy takes a piece and does the same, all the while smiling with his eyes.

When you've both had your fill, he gathers up the other coconuts and puts them into a mesh bag and slings it over his shoulder. You walk beside him as he heads back to the village.

"Tell me a pirate story," you say.

This is the end of your free preview. For more adventures where 'you say which way' the story goes, visit:

YouSayWhichWay.com

More You Say Which Way Adventures

Pirate Island

Volcano of Fire

Between the Stars

Once Upon an Island

In the Magician's House

Secrets of Glass Mountain

Danger on Dolphin Island

The Sorcerer's Maze - Jungle Trek

The Sorcerer's Maze - Adventure Quiz

YouSayWhichWay.com

Made in the USA
Columbia, SC
08 April 2020